Upon the Blood of Her Enemies

DARRAGHA FOSTER

DEDICATION

For Annalisa, who inspired Reggie

ACKNOWLEGMENT

Thanks to Rodney D. Brock for allowing me the use of his song lyrics from My Psychiatrist is a Cattleman. *The words "Choice cut on a china plate" fit the scene so well. And thanks to my daughter, Annalisa Foster, for so regally capturing the spirit of the heroine in this novel — without even knowing it.*

UPON THE BLOOD OF HER ENEMIES

CONTENTS

PROLOGUE

Prior to the events of the heroine of this tale, but before the post-war dust had settled...

The queen was determined from the first to be far more than just a figurehead. A smart woman, she had the gift of sight, which only enhanced her intelligence. Like many post-war survivors, she was always hungry, always on guard and untrusting as hell. She was certain her quick mind and sharp bite were what convinced the council to appoint her as *absolute monarch*. Being pregnant helped too. A viable pregnancy post-war was nothing less than a miracle. Only a person capable of bringing life into the world could rule. It was an odd decree, but one that went unchallenged. It'd been an attempt by the new regime to instill a nurturing heart into power. A mother's love for her people. A firm but gentle hand. Since it was a job that provided shelter and ensured she and her child would not starve, she'd accepted.

After three days living inside the newly constructed royal complex, the nightmares began. Their meaning was clear. Adept at dream interpretation and open to the possibility that humankind was not the bright center of the universe, she recognized the rather testy, spirituous being haunting the compound. Listened to it. Gave its issues credence and voice.

The war had awakened it. Fed it. Now robust and energetic, it had needs. And wants. Truce and reconstruction just plain pissed it off.

It was within the trance-like discussions she held with the spirit who made its home in the center of an ancient puzzle-like construct she saw the wisdom of the council in placing a mother on the throne. It wasn't for the people—it was to control the angry spirit.

"There must be balance," she acknowledged. *Balance, indeed.*

The queen waited until her son was born and weaned, then entered the realm of the spirit of the world to give it one hell of a timeout. Not only a firm hand and boundaries, but also what it needed most…companionship.

In her absence, the council appointed a regent to act in her stead until a suitable replacement could be found. No one suspected the next queen would be the prince. Their spoiled, temperamental, willful prince.

CHAPTER ONE

Evening

Nightmares of blood and defeat crept in during times of rigid wakefulness now. One moment, she focused hard on her trek through hunger, thirst, sweat and muck-covered goggles, and a second later, she became inexplicably lost in a dark abyss of memories and maybes. A long slog through the desert could sap one's strength. Play tricks on the mind. She knew that. She knew all too well.

Delusions made her weak. Weakness made her dead.

At least the trek was all but over. Not her empty belly nor parched throat nor blistered feet would stop dawn from breaking the utter darkness of the desert night.

Come daylight, the journey ended and the battle began.

In the distance the steam-generated electric lights of Ironhedge-Ghillie shone out across the scrap lands like a jewel in the sand. She hunkered down around her fire of dried dung. Dog? Human? She didn't care. It burned. It lit the night and gave subtle warmth.

Her stomach rolled. Anxiety on an empty stomach. She'd taken the specter of starvation to bed before. Truthfully, she'd taken worse into her arms to fill the void of night.

Her stomach ached and sucked the breath from her as it spasmed. It was an ulcer. A bleeding rip in her belly. She knew it. She didn't care. She ignored her aching gut. Her needs didn't matter right now. Only staunching the flow of blood from her twin brother's veins mattered.

That was why she'd made the long haul. That was why she had to win.

Opportunity presented itself when a Long Rider had been thrown from his horse. His neck broken, she'd taken advantage of the situation. Reggie had tucked away the dagger she'd taken off the body before burying him in a shallow grave of stones and scrub. She'd pocketed the knife, some coin and the proclamation of the queen — the call to battle.

As far as she knew, she was the only Red Zone fighter en route to IG. *If I'm the lone contestant from the RZ, then I won't have to kill one of my own.*

Movement caught her gaze. Something small and quick darted about outside the rim of her fire's glow. She retrieved the knife and then extended the blade, poised to dispatch the unwary beastie. Whatever it was that wanted to warm itself by her fire was food. Meat. A little repast to calm her bellyache and renew her strength.

Her aim proved true. She crawled away from her fire to retrieve the still twitching scrap land rodent. Reggie made quick work of dressing the medium-sized rat. She peeled its fur off in one piece, hacked off the tail and feet and scraped away the innards.

She swallowed the heart, warm and raw, whole. She skewered the flesh at the end of her walking stick over the fire.

Almost instantly the delicious odor of char and sizzle of fat rose and misted the dry air. Her mouth watered. Over rat. The heavenly scent attracted others, who like her, were hungry in the night.

She'd watched the pack play in the distance. Dog boys. Canine shapeshifters. They left her alone. She left them alone. Until the magnificent odor of cooked rat attracted their attention.

One of the dog boys approached now. On foot. His gait as a man was as smooth and stealthy as his pads had been playful on the sand.

White-blond hair, unruly and spiked, danced in the firelight. He had the tri-color eyes of his kind. They glowed like little stars. They seemed to have candles lit behind them. Two bluish orbs dancing across the darkness toward her. He walked confidently along the border between light and dark, just inside the glow. He nodded slightly, his mouth in a sly smirk.

There was no rule of etiquette for the sharing of food in the scrap lands. Two travelers in the night generally didn't meet and dine. Unless one fed upon the other.

The rat's fat popped and sizzled. The smell

made her feel heady. Greedy.

"It's too small to share," she called. "I caught it. It's mine." She thought perhaps he was the most alluring male she'd ever laid eyes on. The wildly handsome shapeshifter stepped closer. She smelled his musk. It only added to her hunger.

"Lady's meat brightens this otherwise barren night with promise of quelled desire."

She turned the rat in the flames. "It's my meat."

"There's little game outside the IG. The pack is hungry, but respectful of her hands who caught the rodent. I suggested, perhaps, lady would share if asked nicely."

"Why are you shifters so eloquent in human form? I know you're a wolf-dog under that manskin. Dog boys should be able to catch their own rats. You're stronger and faster on all fours. Go hunt."

"We've had little success of late. It would appear you have obtained the last tasty morsel in the area."

"We both know that's a load of crap," Reggie replied.

The shapeshifter chuckled. The sound of laughter mixed with the scent of cooked meat, and anticipation of ending the specter of starvation, acted like an aphrodisiac upon her senses. She liked this shifter. Women of her zone spoke plainly and openly about such things. She saw no reason to hold her tongue now.

"In another time, in other circumstances, I'd have you," Reggie said. "I'd let you eat of my catch and then I would let you have a taste of something sweeter."

"Boldly spoken for a lone woman, but I understand. In another time, in other circumstances, if I wasn't starving, and we weren't heeding the call of our queen, I would let you take me. There is no shame in allowing a woman such as yourself to ride my cock until we're both spent. The strong thighs of a fighter are very special indeed. Such glories we would find in each other's arms."

"You know what I am then?"

He nodded. "Indeed. I have seen you before. I remember your tattoos." He drew closer to her fire. "In a pit match in Antioch. You won. You're brilliant. I'm also decorated." He displayed the intricate tattoo designs on his right arm.

"I was successful that night." Reggie lifted her staff and held out the sizzling rat flesh to the shifter. "Leave me some."

His fingers deftly peeled away a small strip of rib meat. He blew on it and then popped it into his mouth. "It's no small matter to give a dog boy meat."

"I know your customs, shifter. You've eaten. Now go away and leave me be."

"Thank you, fighter. Your kindness shall be remembered long after I've defeated you in battle."

Reggie didn't reply, though a hundred witty and perhaps egotistical comments rattled through her mind. This wasn't the time nor place to kick doggy butt. *The less he knows of my skills, the stronger my attack will be when it counts. He's just trying to woo me into a little scuffle. Size me up? I don't think so.*

"Go chase your tail."

"I look forward to meeting you again."

She grunted and ate silently as she watched the sensual shapeshifter stroll away into the darkness.

Sleep never really came with her stomach far from full and her mind engaged in naughty thoughts of intercourse with that shiny-eyed shapeshifter.

CHAPTER TWO

Morning

Reggie lowered her head and pulled her hood down to cover her face as she stepped onto the old cattle grate walkway used for foot traffic into the city. The concrete and iron structure had withstood the test of time. The cattle path was a rarity in that it reeked of both the past and future. Not many places still on the grid had ties to the *before times* and the constructs of the second Age of Steam. Reggie had little faith in the new era and its architects, but knew how to work the system — *their system* — and planned on using her cunning to its full advantage.

As her sand and dust-covered mismatched boots clanged against the rusty steel, she realized she could very well be headed toward her last battle. Steam-generated doom. She was good, but how good were the others who had answered the call to arms? How good were the others, who, like her, were desperate enough to commit their very lives for their cause? Causes were for the wealthy and well-fed. Causes weren't something Zoners aspired to achieve. "Have you eaten today?" was the standard greeting in the Zones. For good reason.

Reggie had a cause. One for which she was ready to give her life.

The uneven grate of the cattle ramp under foot reminded her that, against odds a stronger man would fear, she had made it this far. To Ironhedge-Ghillie. On foot. To win.

Would she be queried as to her goal as part of the audition process, or would she have to prove she could kill without flinching? The latter was more her style. Thoughts of having to answer questions produced acid in her belly. She had a rehearsed answer. *I shall pay my brother's debts and see him freed after I'm crowned victor. He's an indentured servant in a Sang brothel. He's too gentle to be a Wasteland blood-whore.*

The IG had too many rules. Part of the audition, she was certain, was to get beyond the gates. Since mostly uncouth periphery dwellers answered the call to battle, their behavior in polite society was no doubt monitored and wagered upon.

Zoners, especially citizens of the Red Zone far to the south, such as herself, generally shied away from civilization with its airships and machinations of the elite and subversive underpinnings of moral decay. In the Zones things could be taken at face value. There were no rules of etiquette or conventions to be applied to their daily lives. Sex was sex. Taxes were levied per breath taken. Food meant life, and no food meant continued struggle. A slave was at the very least, amongst the living. In the city, death didn't necessarily mean dead. Recycling took on a whole new meaning inside the walls of the IG.

The grid shifted a bit underfoot as she ascended. She took another step up the ramp and vocalized a soft *maw,* like a calf calling for its mother. It reminded her of what she was to the ruling class. Meat. Choice cut on a china plate to be grilled and seasoned however *they* wished.

Hot puffs of steam wafted up through the grating from the lower sector where blue-hot turbines powered the city. It was a place both revered and reviled that had not seen a dry day in over a hundred years. Steam power had left everything in a perpetual state of dampness, both below and above. She and her RZ kin called Ironhedge-Ghillie a "wrinkle-free zone" since steam had been used to press out wrinkles in the old days. Ironhedge-Ghillie's sins were neatly pressed into hiding, though everyone knew they were there. Like a piss-stain on the front of a gentleman's trousers, it wasn't mentioned, no matter how obvious. That's what IG was, one big classy, wrinkle-free piss-stain on the trousers of humanity. Although one might argue that, with the heavy recycling programs of IG, the piss-stain also graced most of the city's *in*humanity too.

The assaulting hot puffs of steam left her wet and shivering, but this was the way of things in the city. Steam came first. Steam made the city and its unique opportunities, well, *opportunities*. She'd been born into a world where steam ruled, and where to purposely douse a fire used to generate steam for another was a capital crime.

Reggie figured she'd have been walled up, beheaded, or drowned years ago had she not been born a Zoner. And a fighter. Therein lay her value. Thereby her transgressions and petty crimes had been overlooked in favor of her ability in a pit fight. She didn't revere steam. She revered her flesh more. Her right fist, especially.

* * * *

The ornate brass clock above the ancient wrought iron gate struck one o'clock as she passed through the first checkpoint. There were four "wayfarer's stations" into IG. Each had an attendant and "guest relations advocates." There were hundreds of regulations for visitors. Failure to comply meant public censure, which she was sure city dwellers enjoyed, the sick bastards, or personal encoding forbidding city entrance in perpetuity. Reggie had been dreading this moment since leaving the Zone. More than leaving home, more than leaving her brother a slave to salacious blood-sipping buggers, more than crossing the Wastelands on foot, entering IG was both the bravest and most frightening act of her life.

The reward for surviving the arena was worth any hardship.

Zoners said only fools and victors ever made the trek to the arena at the heart of the central city. She was no fool.

The scar above her left eye ached. It acted like a signal when she found herself in tense situations. Entering the grand central city of Ironhedge-Ghillie had it pulsating like the last breaths of a fish out of water. She rubbed her fingers across the healed flesh to relax the palpable pain assaulting her. It was a thick one, unsightly and outlawed. Open displays of having suffered a violent life weren't considered polite. One of the regulations. Outbursts, fighting, protests, any display of aggression, were outlawed by royal decree. Scarring and bruises, even if from an accident, were to be kept hidden.

Reggie never tried to hide her scar, though it bisected her eyebrow and radiated out like a spider's web at the corner of her bright hazel left eye. She'd sewn the wound up herself with plasticized thread she'd found half-buried along the shore. "Floss." An unusual name for an item made of a substance from a time before the Age of Steam. From the before-times. Before the war.

She felt as if she had a large red arrow hovering over her head, indicating she'd once suffered the consequences of rage. Her hood did little to obscure it, and there was no use trying to arrange her locks to cover the blemished flesh. She'd long ago given up trying to keep her unruly hair in place. She'd gone to an extreme to keep it out of her way short of going bald, which was always an option. An old woman with skin the color of tar, who rapped on a cook pot to make music, had taught her how to wrap her hair to create what had once been called "dreads." Reggie liked the name of the style. She liked to incite "dread" in her opponents.

Lost in thought, Reggie nearly stumbled on the switchback cattle grate as she reached her destination. She cleared her throat before the high desk of Wayfarer Station Number One.

The attendant didn't even look up from his scrawl-pad — a steam-powered device that he wrote upon with a fingernail cap that instantaneously transmitted the data through a wire to the Grand Archive at the heart of the city by way of taps and clicks, which were then translated into words. She knew she was about to be "memorialized." Every Zoner knew about the info-dumps on every heartbeat in IG. It was an accepted form of technology, because it relied on steam to generate it. Whip out a surviving old-fashioned typewriter and one would likely be drawn and quartered. Use the original version of Morse code and surely the sky itself would fall.

Technology powered by steam is pure. It was framed on the wall behind the attendant. Not looking up or acknowledging her in any way, the attendant asked, "Male or female?"

Reggie replied softly. Very softly. "Female." She wasn't dressed as a female, and city code dictated that lone females weren't allowed to move unaccompanied within the outer walls.

The attendant glanced up through the steam emanating from his scrawl-pad. "Human or hybrid?"

Reggie leaned in, trying to keep their conversation private. "Hybrid."

"Hybrid ability?"

"Visual." Reggie didn't have to divulge the

nature of her hybrid abilities, except by the single word catch-phrases allowed via the Mutations Equality Act enacted in Year Two, postwar. Visual, auditory, tactile, projection, detection…one word was all a recording agent could obtain.

"Zoner?"

Reggie withheld a snide remark. *Do I look like a Wastelander, you moron?* "Red."

"Long journey to find work, assuming that's the advent of your trek. We have need of a few Sanguinarians at the hospital, and we can always use more Disposals. Oh, you're not an airship pilot, are you? The fleet is always looking for new recruits, and the pay is quite good, I hear." He paused, taking a thoughtful look at her. "Though if you're here to ply your pillowing skills, I'm afraid you'll have to audition for placement in a brothel." He nodded toward a partition to his left. She saw a grease-stained feather mattress through rips in the curtains draped over the wooden frame. "Or perhaps you're simply another strong back and seek the hard labor but high rewards of the underground…"

"I'm not a vampire, nor am I a garbage eater," Reggie replied. "And I'm not a whore or shovel jockey."

"Then what do you have to offer IG? And who, may I ask, is your escort?"

Here it goes. I've crossed hundreds of miles of crap-land on foot and worked my whole life for this moment. I can do it. I can say it. "I can fight. And I need no escort."

"Fighting is illegal. Any contact sport from the old system has been outlawed by the queen.

Wrestling, boxing, martial arts…all illegal."

Reggie nodded. "All the same, I'm very good at what I do."

The attendant tapped nervously on his pad. Something quick. Two words, maybe. Reggie hoped it wasn't "kill her." He cocked his head and held very still for a moment. He wore an earpiece. Someone controlled his decisions from behind the scenes. Someone else watched her. Right then. Right there.

The attendant nodded as if Reggie had spoken to him. She hadn't. Another sign that the scrivener wasn't acting alone.

He straightened his posture, and very abruptly said, "I'm giving you a three-day pass to the outer city. If you intend to travel beyond your lodgings for any reason, you must pay for an escort. They dress similarly in black. They work on a connected grid, so any one of them can summon another for you. As long as you're accompanied, you're within the law."

"Fine. Whatever." She held out her hand as the attendant used an air-injection wand to insert a tracking device into the soft tissue between her thumb and index finger. The instrument's brass flashed in the dim light. The pattern carved into it was well-worn from countless jabs into the hands of city-goers. The forefinger and thumb depressions of the attendant had etched themselves onto the device.

"Now we just need to wait for the data stream," he said. "You do know what that is, don't you, Zoner?"

"I know what a data stream is. We don't call it

that in the Zone, but it's all the same thing. You've been at this job for a long time, huh?"

"Yes. I'm lucky to have it," the attendant said. "How can you tell?"

"Your wand is worn about the edges as if it were molded to fit your hand."

"It's the tool of my trade. And you, Zoner, are very perceptive." He leaned forward. "A smart trait in a fight, no?"

"I'd like to stay at the Zeppelin Hostel," Reggie said. The Zeppelin Hostel was an enclave for ex-pat Zoners living in the city. At least she wouldn't feel so alone and out of place with her own kind.

The attendant read the symbols as they appeared on his scrawl-pad. "You're a disease-free hybrid female."

"I'm aware of that."

The attendant made a slight motion with his right hand. "These escorts will guide you to the Clockworx Tower. There's no room at the ZH just now."

Reggie felt a hand against her arm. She bristled at the touch. She turned her head to find two identically dressed "guest" escorts standing behind her. She wrinkled her nose. She didn't like their type. Pseudo dandies. Dead men dressed in high class attire. They gave her the willies. Each wore a purple velvet jacket, beige riding breeches, a top hat, and a monocle. They were dressed according to the queen's personal tastes. A ridiculous uniform for a ridiculous ruler.

"Thanks for the escort, but I can manage."

The escorts shook their heads and, in unison, replied, "No unaccompanied females in the outer rim."

Reggie tried a second time to free herself of her escorts. "I can take care of myself. I know where the Clockworx Tower is. I can see it from here. I've never used the services of *Pseudos* before and I see no reason to begin now."

She realized how bigoted her statement sounded. Pseudos couldn't help what they were. They were epic fails. Reanimated, reconstructed, and recycled. They were used for labor and in the brothels. Given a task, they did it well. Given an abstract thought, they basically self-destructed. In the Zones they were called "Sortas" for "sort of human" or "Kindas" as in "kind of human."

"It isn't permitted. For your safety. The queen commands it." The lead escort squeezed his fingers.

Reggie cast an annoyed glance at the attendant. "Really? Pseudos? A girl can't even get a real man to show her around the place these days?" There was no response from him or the purple velvet-dressed, top-hat wearing creatures next to her. "I can handle myself. Do you think for one moment I couldn't beat down an attacker?"

The attendant chuckled. "The idea is to make it so there is no reason to 'beat anyone down,' as you so brutally put it. This is a conflict-free zone for a very good reason."

Reggie opened her mouth, ready to begin a debate, when she was interrupted by the rambunctious leap and bound of the dog boy. The shifter.

"There you are!" He darted up the ramp and nearly toppled Reggie in greeting. "She's with me. I'll escort her. No need for one of these fine reanimated gentlemen to go out of their way for her." He took Reggie by the shoulders. "Come along now, darling. The Clockworx isn't far."

Reggie raised a questioning eyebrow at the shifter, but didn't balk at his well-timed rescue. She moved past the wayfarer station, grateful for the company of a living creature.

"Pseudos give me the creeps. Thank you for the escort. Silly rule."

"They're none too fond of us, either," said the dog boy. "Some say they will rise against the fully living. Have you heard this rumor in the RZ?"

"I've heard it all. Are we even now? I gave you meat and you give me escort?"

"If you'd like to look at it that way, yes. I was rather hoping we could get to know each other—"

Reggie cut him off. "Before I rip your lungs out through your ribcage in the arena?"

"Yes, exactly. You intrigued me in Antioch, and last night, when I realized it was you...well, I'm a fan."

Reggie didn't pull away as he took her arm. "I don't give autographs."

The shifter squeezed her elbow. "What about fellatio?"

Reggie laughed off the comment and quickly changed the subject. *Sure, I'm attracted to him. Who wouldn't be? He's a freaking feral beast in manskin. He's also my opponent.* "You answered the call, then?"

"I fight for my pack."

"To what end? What reward does your pack seek?" The shifter laughed so hard it drew the attention of others. Reggie quickly pulled him aside. "Don't be so loud. Stealth is important. Especially in a place like this."

A uniformed peace officer approached. Reggie pushed the shifter against the brick wall of the foyer they'd entered and engaged him in a long kiss.

"Eh…none of that here. Move along. You young people have no sense of decorum. And you, girl. Cover that scar. It's not allowed." The officer sauntered away.

"Not a fan of the law, my dear?"

Reggie pulled from his embrace. With difficulty. "No. My call to battle arrived via the broken neck of a Long Rider. I prefer to avoid questions regarding the situation."

"I do love a woman who skirts the law," the shifter said. "And one who uses me as an impromptu distraction. Well…I say we continue the distraction in your room."

I don't need a private room. I'm a woman of the Red Zone. I could wear you thin right here. Right now. But I know better. "Not right now. Good doggy."

Reggie stepped back into the throng and hub-bub of the IG. They mixed into the hustle and bustle and great cacophony of bodies milling about, the sounds of which had been shielded at the wayfarer station. She noticed the dynamic audible change immediately. The station had been relatively quiet.

The stainless-steel arch at the proper entrance to the city shone like the tips of waves on the ocean, and she was pretty sure she heard a hum—as if electricity passed through it. She'd heard the hum of an electrical current before. Steam-generated electricity wasn't yet commonplace, but it was used here and there. The Red Zone's medical center had it for three hours a day. The day she'd broken her wrist in a pit fight she'd been taken there. Most Zoners felt safer using folk remedies and neighborhood healers. A trip to the medical center was a crap shoot of care. She was lucky her wrist had been set properly and that she'd lived to fight another day. The surgeon said he'd inserted a pin to repair the broken bone.

She'd later visualized using it as a weapon. Since men in Wasteland fight pits had been known to wield their own bones as implements of battle, why not a steel pin from her wrist? Everything could be used as a weapon. From the little metal shards woven into her hair to her womanhood. Sex was a powerful weapon in its own right.

Reggie reached out to touch the vibrating steel frame. Her fingers reacted to the cold metallic tactile sensation. It wasn't one she was accustomed. Something this smooth and large could only have been fabricated in the before-times, or by a very skilled city craftsman. She tried to discern its structural source. It appeared entirely solid, forged from one piece of steel.

"Well, that's interesting," she whispered.

"You're dawdling."

"I always liked building things as a kid. This structure fascinates me. Do you know its origins?"

"I was born here. Not in this section, and admittedly, outside the wall, but I have crossed this path many times. The structure was created from pieces of a great arch that once stood across the harbor."

"There is no harbor here."

"The inland sea and its tributaries dried up with the climate change postwar. The salt flats not too far from the west gate are all that remain of the port."

"That's interesting," Reggie replied. "There is nothing as smooth as this arch in the RZ."

The Zones were gritty and bleak. There was no façade or veneer of civility. Reggie believed the old-times phrase was "third world." Little infrastructure, few services, and tribal rule. Not so in the city.

Women in long skirts and bustles, carrying delicate umbrellas but wearing sidearms and escorted by black leather-clothed males, filled the street. It was a rainbow of color, and a spectacle like none other. It seemed to be more of a parade than a marketplace. And everywhere the moist, hot breath of steam filled the air. Vendors with warmer trays of hot foods the likes she'd never smelled before, priests offering the blessing of steam, fire-starters and water bearers, and, on every flat surface, the reminders of days past. Placards, posted high and low, and probably overlooked by those who saw them every day, told the tale of the second age. *This city has been built upon the ashes of technology's downfall. Only steam can save the world. Fossil fuels and atomic energy equal death.*

Happy little reminders.

Reggie didn't own a dress. Never had. She was dressed for the road, and assumed the only clean spot on her body was the area underneath the goggles she'd worn while trekking across the wilderness. She didn't do mirrors. She hadn't looked at her own reflection in months. *My appearance must be frightful and manly to city dwellers.* Not a female in sight wore pants or carried anything larger than their head. Reggie carried a pack about the size of a hound dog. It smelled about the same as an old, wet dog too.

I'm so underdressed for this place. These women are more colorful than wild peacocks and budgies. She chastised herself for thinking she was lesser than the peacocks of Ironhedge-Ghillie. *Stop it, Reg. Quit comparing yourself.* She shook off the aura of inequality. *I'm here to fight. That's what I do. I don't need lacy undergarments or crocheted handbags to prove my worth.* She dropped her hood, deliberately trying to display her scar and unusual hair. *I know my worth. I'm a victor. And that's why I'm here.* From the hurried steps and covered gasps, the polite society of the city knew she was there too.

✴ ✴ ✴ ✴

A good fighter observes.

A good fighter learns from the actions of those around her.

Reggie wasn't sure what she could learn from eavesdropping on the conversation between a well-dressed woman speaking distinctly with a man busy wringing a chicken's neck, but the contrived and seemingly scripted nature of it amused her. The buyer was apparently unhappy with the last bird and wanted to discuss the matter with the seller, who was busy preparing a hen for another customer.

The buyer shielded her eyes and nostrils from the killing. "I must have larger breasts and plumper thighs."

Yeah, we all need larger breasts and plumper thighs, sister. Reggie kept her opinions to herself. It wouldn't do to interrupt the conversation with a snort of laughter. *Be happy you had a chicken at all, woman. And don't fuss with the butcher. Give him what-for and then he'll pull out the plump birds. She doesn't know how to haggle! Oh, wait…haggling is restricted.*

So taken with the mob, she nearly tripped over one of the hundreds of steam pipes jutting up from the cobblestone street. She thought their shape provocatively phallic.

"So, who made steam vents shaped like giant penises? Was that the queen's idea?" she asked.

"Ah, yes. You like those? If you're aroused, and still don't wish to find pleasure with me, I'm sure we can find you a dolly for a bit of heave-ho in an alleyway."

Reggie coughed. A dolly was a low-class male prostitute. Her brother's predicament was one step below that. "No, thank you. I don't play with dollies. And who says I'm not going to take you?"

The shifter chuckled. "I live for that moment."

Traffic grew dense and more varied the farther they proceeded toward the Clockworx Tower. It was difficult to get a good look at the lovely old buildings. Everyone knew the city was full of secrets. Children's rhymes and folklore were thin disguises. IG had layers. Layers and layers of history mortared with blood and constraint.

At the heart of Ironhedge-Ghillie was the arena.

The labyrinth. Citizens gathered along the outer walls of the arena to make offerings, mourn, wed — even give birth. It was the only place in the whole of the world where dreams could become reality. If you were fast and strong.

The labyrinth represented life, death, freedom and fortune. It held both physical and mystical properties never discussed above a whisper. It'd become the venue for contact sports officially forbidden, yet not-so-secretly engaged in. That's where Reggie fit in.

As she caught her first glimpse of the white marble walls encasing the arena, she finally felt that one emotion she refused to acknowledge since she'd serendipitously made the decision to fight.

Fear.

It puckered her bowels and rolled her stomach. Her palms sweated.

She was sure her heart would beat through her chest.

CHAPTER THREE

Ironhedge-Ghillie was a hub of deviance and violence tucked under a banner of peace just like a blood-engorged flea hiding in the lining of a silk frock. Conflict may have been outlawed, but it secretly ruled. The symbol of the queen was everywhere. Reggie tried not to laugh at the image chosen as the symbol of the monarchy. A purple hen standing atop a brass and silver filigree pocketwatch, the bird's feet scratching at the crystal. She knew it meant the queen had defeated time, place and circumstances to become the first male queen of the world. Part of the trinity of Time, Steam, and Queen. Viktor, the queen, had been a clever, clever princeling. He knew the law. He used it to catapult himself onto the throne.

The founder's council had decreed only those who could bring life had a compassionate enough heart to rule IG and the Zones. Short of becoming a necromancer or resurrectionist, bringing life into the world had to be done the old-fashioned way—by giving birth. Viktor's mother had disappeared into the arena on a pilgrimage, leaving her son behind. It was said she'd given her life over to holy steam to usher in a new era for her people. Reggie didn't have an ear for stories. She liked facts. Folktales were nothing but poetic lies in her opinion.

The prince became queen when he came of age.

By giving birth.

By caesarean.

The law-speakers acquiesced to his ingenuity. He'd met the letter of the law and fulfilled the necessary requirements.

Queen Viktor stood a powerfully built man with a full beard, who oft-times displayed his more male characteristics quite openly. He held court in a codpiece of soft leather, antique pilot's goggles and a wool scarf flanked by his prized borzoi. He urinated off the balcony of the Great House—his palace. There was no doubt he was all man—one who'd taken the ripe uterus of a woman and had had it implanted into his body with the aid and skill of a great physician and even greater bioengineer.

The baby grew.

And Viktor ascended the throne three days after the birth.

His first decree? To outlaw contact sports while secretly developing a vast under-society of gamers and blood games. Not to mention it became unlawful to disturb the peace of the city—in any manner. Even haggling over the price of a chicken. And Wastelanders were considered freaks? Reggie didn't think so.

The front desk of the Clockworx was made of steel and decorated with broken clock parts. It was an on-going theme. "Overcome the ravages of time with effort," had been a mantra of the postwar years. The face of a clock was almost as sacred as steam.

A mildly attractive older gentleman greeted Dog Boy. "Well, bless my heart. Good to see you again, my friend." He held out his hand to the shifter. "Your pack is in the game room. I think they're all drunk on half-ale. Who have you brought me here?" He released Dog Boy's hand and extended it to Reggie. "Welcome to Clockworx Tower." He too wore a monocle and waistcoat. Faded and well-mended, it hearkened back to the glory days of IG before the freaks had come out to play, *and rule*.

"Lady, I shall leave you to your preparations." The shifter leaned down and kissed her cheek. "I won't be far, should you need anything. Anything at all." He winked at the desk clerk. "Treat her right, my friend. She's very special."

"Star treatment all the way," he replied.

Reggie shook the desk clerk's hand, her mind unable to focus on anything save the touch of Dog's lips against her cheek. Even as the clerk passed her hand through a device that reminded her of an old-fashioned toaster turned on its side, her mind wandered.

The device shot out a slip of paper with her room number and lock code emblazoned upon it. "You're on sub-level ten, room seventeen. Your dining area is on sub-level nine. No food in your room, please. How will you be paying today? You don't appear to have enough credits in your account."

Reggie took a deep breath to clear her mind as she reached inside her leather jacket and then removed a small strip of palladium. "Will this cover it?"

The desk clerk pulled out a jeweler's eye piece and held the metal strip out to examine it. "This is real. How'd an outlander like you come by this? And why would you use it to stay here? Why carry something so valuable with you instead of assimilating its worth into your credit account?"

Reggie leaned over the counter. "I won it in a fight."

"Ah, I see. You're here to audition then," the clerk surmised.

Reggie nodded. "I'm here to win."

"I find this form of payment acceptable. Please proceed to your chamber. Do try the vegetable hash at dinner service," the clerk replied. "It has been carefully prepared for our special guests." He waggled his right eyebrow and emphasized his words.

Fighter code. Has to be. Is "vegetable hash" code for fight master? She didn't press.

The pack had taken over a game table in the lobby across from the elevators. Her new friend watched her, a sly smile on his lips. Reggie didn't look away. That was a sign of weakness. Strong eye contact was the first move in an offensive. She nodded. A greeting of sorts. She couldn't look away if she'd wanted to. Those eyes of his...those glowing eyes...

He acknowledged her ever so slightly by a slight

lift of his left eyebrow.

Reggie flashed him a shy smile. *What the fuck am I doing? Playing demure with a dog boy? Holy steam...get your head in the game, girl!* She glanced his way again. In his purely human form, he was far from the colloquialism of "dog boy." He was clearly all man. Rugged, yet lithe. Sexy as the most beautiful vampire in a Sang brothel—and that said a lot. The Sangs radiated beauty. It was how they lured their victims—or their customers if a brothel servant. Dog Boy here...with his tri-colored eyes and blond hair. Gorgeous. His height and weight did not make him grotesque. Certainly he had a hundred pounds and ten inches on her, but he was far from muscle-bound. He could move quickly, deliberately—without falter or imbalance. He could probably go all night. *I could make him howl. And think how agile and strong any offspring we produce would be. I can see our children running a gauntlet someday, their bellies full and faces washed because we have won the big prizes and retired from the pits. Good gods holy steam, I can't think this way. There is no future beyond the pits. Or the arena. I am a fighter.* She tucked her fantasies deep into the farthest reaches of her almost impenetrable heart and moved on.

She'd always been attracted to their kind. Very masculine, canine hybrids. From full-on male form to all-fours, snarl and tail, she liked their style. In their halfway point between wolf or dog and man—some kind of mishmash of man and beast—their intelligence quota wasn't over the top, but in manskin, they were brilliant and incredibly appealing.

Animal instincts and passions combined with,

when in human form, poetic verse and an almost Sang-like intelligence. *And there he stands, that man with the tri-colored eyes who sweet-talked me into feeding him in a survival situation and saved my ass from a zombie escort. Hello, handsome…*

Focus! She turned her attention to the task at hand. Room. Shower. Food. As she scanned the placard over the lift to find her destination queue, she realized, sadly, there would be little chance for love this trip. Reggie hadn't had an orgasm by someone else's hand for quite a while, and after she'd been billed for a nocturnal climax via a dream, she had resisted the urge. Damn body sensors tracked everything. It still irritated her that she'd had to pay two credits for an orgasm, which occurred unbidden, while she was asleep. *Must have been a doozey to have set off the sensor tracking my vitals. It's not that the ruling class wants to keep track of my health and welfare,* she assured herself. *They keep us lo-jacked with sensors to know when we've starved to death. Another blessing of steam-generated techno drivel.* Between training and gathering enough food for herself and her brother, and deciding very quickly to follow the call after finding the body of the rider, there had been no time for sex. It'd been a long time, indeed. *After I win, I'll go to the brothel and work out some of my pent-up tension.*

* * * *

"I like her," the shifter said to one of the pack as he waited for his cup to be filled by a guest attendant.

"Dangerous to desire the company of another

fighter, Hundi, my friend. What do you intend to do? Bed her, then kill her in the arena?"

"Yes. That works for me. Though, I believe I'd miss her if she weren't in my arms every night. That could be an exploitable weakness on my part."

"Use your lust to the best advantage, brother. She's a comely female, and Red Zone women are always most passionate in love and war."

The shifter, Hundi, nodded. "I'll let you know how it goes after I win." He drank from his cup thoughtfully. His breed was educated. Oft-times intellectual. At least when in manskin. The animal had its own knowledge and skills. The challenge before him had certainly taken him to baser thoughts—memories of coppery blood and steaming entrails—of the sweetest music—the final rattled breath of his opponent as he drowned in his own blood. *Good things, these.* The howl of the hounds rang in his ears. But her scent overshadowed and filled all his senses. He could smell the dirt of the road from her boots and the moistness of her quim when she glanced his way. Her sweat was an aphrodisiac. He wanted her. He wanted inside her. It frightened him how desperately he wanted to catch her eye. She was a weapon in her own right. Her ripeness called to him. She was of breeding age. They could mate. Raise children. Run their own pit fight or training center. *Oh, this woman—I must have her.*

* * * *

A hollow, tinny-sounding bell chimed, and the elevator appeared in a puff of steam. Reggie patted her jacket. It, like her hair and skin, was moist from the over-abundance of steam. *Makes me almost miss the desert regions.* She felt uncomfortable from the perpetual dampness of the air. *I'm suffocating. The air is so thick here. How do these people breathe?*

The attendant smiled like a brainwashed zealot and ushered her into the elevator. He pulled the grate closed and then shifted the lever to sub-level ten. A flurry of steam puffed up from beneath the ornate car, and their descent commenced. Reggie had never ridden in one before. The ride was much slower than she'd anticipated. *What does one do while standing in a six foot square steel box with a man in a faded tux, pulling various levers, gaze fixed on the steam output?*

"Excuse me, sir…but how long is the ride to sub-level ten?"

"Seventeen minutes, fifty-three seconds. May I interest you in the latest audio broadcast from Queen Viktor?"

Reggie tried not to snort. "No, no thanks."

The elevator operator turned to face her. "May I interest you in a short but fulfilling sexual encounter?"

"Here?" Reggie asked. "You're an elevator-operating whore?"

"Not the nicest way of putting it, but yes. My designation is OneTwelve." He pointed to his brass name badge. "This job is purely ornamental and quite boring. I'm lucky to have it, of course, but the pay is terrible. If you're concerned about being taxed, the queen condones such niceties for visiting

Zoners or Wastelanders. No tax. Plus that, the tips are much better when I give a rider a screaming orgasm. I'm a skilled lover. I can sense in you the need for release too. Perhaps your quim was stimulated by the sight of the pack in the game room? I can smell their musk. Sexy beasts. Or perhaps it was only one of them who entices you so."

Reggie didn't object to the idea. She had a few credits and seventeen minutes to kill. "You, sir…are very perceptive. How much?"

"From which Zone do you hail?"

"Red."

"Ah, Red Zone women are on special this week. I can give you oral pleasure for two credits, or add genital to genital contact for another one-half. Would you like to see my bill of health? We have only fifteen minutes and seventeen seconds remaining. I estimate we will need the entire timespan for you to achieve full satisfaction."

She'd bought sex before. Sometimes it was good. Sometimes it wasn't. After a big win, it was easy to justify a few credits on a bit of quimsticking. Buying it was sure easier than marking time for the formalities of having a monogamous relationship. The Zones weren't family friendly. Marriages were rare. The license to wed was an average cost of five years' salary for most folk. Socializing? Dating? Even masturbation? Recorded. Taxed. Heavily.

"Yeah, all right. Oral."

"It'll take the edge off," the operator said.

"Why would you say that?"

"You're here to fight, aren't you? So far all the citizen guests on sub-level ten are combat auditioners."

"How many have you ferried to sub-level ten?"

OneTwelve laughed. "Not as many as last time. It's believed the Long Rider failed to circumnavigate the Zones. He's dead or in hiding from his term of service. The message didn't get out. The old telegraph system should be restored. Much more efficient than sending out man and horse with decrees. Hold out your hand, please."

Reggie held out her hand. "Do you have a scanner for the credits? I don't see a toaster-style one, and I'm not carrying any currency." A lie. She had a second strip of palladium. But not for sex.

"Olive Picker. Old style. I hope that's all right."

She nodded. Olive Picker scanners had been banned after the second outbreak of a viral skin infection had been linked to their usage. The box scanners—the toasters—didn't actually make contact with flesh. The Olive Pickers did. Even the identification tag inserted into the web of her hand was vaporous. No contact required to insert or read it.

She'd heard that the "breaking of the skin" method of payment had come about as a way to encourage citizens to stop squandering their money in the reign of the former queen. Pain was the deterrent to frivolity. It hadn't worked out well. Certainly citizens had spent less, but the vendors of the time also suffered. And then came the infection. It spread like leprosy.

"Have you cleaned it?" Reggie asked. "I'm old enough to remember the illness associated with OPs."

OneTwelve held out a sealed alcohol prep pad.

"I'll clean it in front of you. You may disrobe unless you want me to pleasure you through your breeches."

Reggie wiggled her fingers, getting tired of holding out her hand. "Just get it over with."

The Olive Picker scanner was no longer than a quill or, using an even rarer object for comparison, a ballpoint pen. A pump at its top deployed a small, delicate metal claw with slightly curved tips. It really did resemble an antique gourmet's instrument for removing olives from a skinny jar without spilling the contents. This device, however, read the implanted commerce chip all citizens carried in the bit of flesh between thumb and index finger.

The claws touched her hand lightly and then poked through, just barely breaking the skin. The magnetic reaction of chip to claw buzzed slightly. The operator withdrew the instrument and checked a digital read-out along its side.

"Two credits received."

Reggie unfastened her breeches and leaned back into the corner of the elevator. "Go ahead."

The operator dropped to his knees and quickly freed her of her heavy cotton duct riding breeches. Not that she had a horse or mule…they were just the only pants she owned.

The mood wasn't conducive to sexual fulfillment. Thirteen minutes in an elevator with a stranger's tongue on her snatch wasn't what she called a seduction. However, OneTwelve had style. And quite obviously, two tongues.

"You're a hybrid." Reggie moaned, squirming as OneTwelve lapped her clitoris and probed her internally at the same time.

"As are you."

Reggie closed her eyes and relaxed enough to allow the freakishly delightful tension spreading through her body to swell. Like velvet sandpaper on the back of a burrowing snake, OneTwelve's tongues earned their two credits. It wasn't customary to reach out to hold a paid sex partner, to kiss him or spoon afterward. She couldn't help herself. She grabbed his head and slammed it to her privates as she achieved orgasm.

He pulled away, his face wet with her nectar. "Seven minutes to spare. You certainly were ardent. Perhaps we'll meet again."

Modesty cast aside, Reggie rested in the corner, breeches at her ankles, pussy still exposed and throbbing. She wanted more. "Man, I needed that. We could do it in seven minutes."

"Intercourse? You don't have enough credits. Low balance," OneTwelve replied.

"You've got a lot to offer a woman. I can see it in your uniform trousers." Reggie hiked up her breeches.

"I do. I'm thick and long, and as you surmised, being a hybrid, quite talented, but I only fill paying customers. Maybe after you win a fight we can reunite. Ah, here we are, your floor." He pulled the elevator gate open and bowed slightly. "Thank you for staying at the Clockworx."

Reggie sauntered out of the elevator, reading the dimly-lit corridor signs for room seventeen. "No, *thank you*. Best elevator ride I've ever had."

"I aim to please!" He waggled his long, forked tongue at her.

Reggie giggled. "Snake boy."

He smiled as he closed the gate. He was gone in a puff of steam.

Reggie felt a rather confident sway in her step. The short but fulfilling sexual encounter had done her a world of good.

The corridor was clean, in a funky institutional way, and the doors were padded on the outside with heavy brocade fabric riveted with brass tacks. Room seventeen was halfway down the hall on the left. Steam lamps flickered every five feet or so. The hotel floor had a classy feel to it. At one time it must have been top-of-the-line.

She was dusty and smelled of the road. It hadn't seemed to bother the elevator operator, but it bothered her to be so grimy in such a sterile place. The fragrance of vinegar and bleach wafted about, only adding to the assault on her senses — most of which she knew emanated from her own body.

Her room wasn't so awful. It had a small water closet with a steam shower, a bed, a table with a worship center, and a speaker box. She flipped the programming chart atop the box. Most of the selections were speeches by the queen. There were one or two audio programs related to travel within the outer city, and one on the Clockworx itself.

A single red light flashed on the speaker box. She'd seen that before — the Zones had something similar. It was the call to prayer.

In IG, it wasn't as much a call to worship as it was a mandatory reminder to appreciate the reconstruction of the city after the war. The worship center was something developed by the city advocates who'd placed all the placards in the square, and to some extent, all over the Zones as well.

She wasn't religious. She didn't revere steam, own a clock, or attend services. Reggie didn't have faith in time or energy. Her faith rested in the strength of her fists.

The signal's flash grew in intensity and the steam connector rattled as pressure built within. She unhooked the iron cap and slid it just far enough to allow a small amount of steam to escape. She glanced at the speaker box. The red light had dimmed. Reggie placed her palms against the table on either side of the steamy flow and took on the position of a supplicant. She knew the drill. All Zoners knew how to genuflect to the power of steam. Most, like her, just went through the motions when forced to worship.

The brass dial on the worship panel shot up to the number six on a scale of ten for her sincerity level. She was adept at fooling sensor panels. Her true measure of sincerity was negative six. This was where a life in the Zones paid off. Living on the fringe of the Wasteland could cause a person to become highly adaptable. Adaptability was key when bluffing sensors.

The steam puffed at her, increasing in heat and density. Reggie closed her eyes and allowed it to envelope her.

The entire call to prayer lasted less than a minute. It was a minute out of her life she'd never regain. That annoyed her.

I could never do this eight times a day. Eight freaking times a day. From queen to underground laborers, every citizen of Ironhedge-Ghillie observed the union of steam and time. *I hope the call to prayer bypasses the arena. That would never do. I wouldn't cease battle to pray, nor would I allow my opponents to participate in such nonsense.*

She rubbed her palms together to free them of the tingle of the sincerity sensor and then recapped the connector.

Stripped of her clothing, her body was a shade lighter than her face and arms. Road dirt. Soot. Ash. Sweat. *Shower. Now.* Hot water. *If ever I were to worship steam, it'd be for this one blessing. Hot water.*

After five days on foot through terrain better suited for hooves than poorly shod feet, the pulsating rush of cleansing water felt magnificent. The Clockworx even supplied some personal hygiene supplies. Tooth powder and brush, a comb and soap. *A comb through my hair? I don't think so.*

Reggie watched the detritus of her trek roll off her body and down the drain. She scrubbed her feet, hoping to rid them of the calluses of too-small boots versus desert travel. The hot water penetrated her mass of dreads, and she massaged her scalp. If any fleas or other insects had taken refuge in her hair, they were bound to be drowned.

She soaped under her breasts and scraped away layers of sand and sweat from under her arms. Her privates reacted to the cascade of hot water, and her thoughts turned again to the skillful tongue of OneTwelve. Or better yet, that sexy dog boy wearing manskin. Aggressive, passionate sex with that fighter Dog Boy. Though she had just felt the tremor of sexual release, the thought of the shifter's large body atop hers, his girth inside her, his mouth on hers and his hands on her breasts, made her body respond appropriately. She wanted him. Now. Any physical contact would have to happen before their entry into the arena. After that—death was the only constant. Still, there was a part of her—a miniscule part, that wished love would conquer all.

The shower shut off after ten minutes. She could have spent another hour under the hot spray. Her belly objected. It was time to eat. She hadn't had a substantial meal in days.

She depressed the call button by the door. "Hey, when's supper around here?"

A mechanical voice replied in a short, terse manner. "Dining hall two, dinner service has commenced."

Reggie patted the button. "Thanks." *On to the vegetable hash and hopefully my audition.*

CHAPTER FOUR

Without the camouflage of dirt, grime and soot, she felt more vulnerable than she had since entering IG. Even the shifter's disarming nature hadn't affected her as much as losing her grungy shield. At least her clothes were still covered in road filth.

There was no time to get comfortable and enjoy a leisurely meal. She needed to eat, hopefully make contact with the fight master and maybe get some shut-eye if she could. She wasn't sure when she'd last slept soundly. Never?

The dining hall had a poured concrete floor with drain holes every twelve feet. Hose bibs stuck out from the wall, two per side. She assumed the cleaning crew must literally hose the room down at night. It was possible the dining hall served several purposes. *I don't want to know the other uses of this room. I'm not asking.*

There were corner shadows—always a place of

concern to a fighter. She'd avoid them and any perils they might bring. Shadows could be her friend or enemy in a fight. Today, the unknown wasn't her ally. Especially with the freak show populating the room. A couple Sangs—the vampire class—gulped down the red stuff and laughed it up in the back of the room at a wet bar. Some dog boys sniffed around the protein table, and several other tough customers were in line at the buffet.

Reggie swallowed hard, stopping herself from a quick reach-out to cop a feel of her new friend, the dog boy as he passed by. He had it going on in his full male state. From his blondish hair and piercing multi-colored eyes to his firm calf muscles and ample bulge, she figured he was about the best she'd ever seen. *Sexually I could wear him thin. Oh, how I could take him. We might end up with broken ribs, but sex with him would be so worth it.*

There weren't any dog girls. The hybrid werewolves took human mates. Daughters were always born human hybrids with varying abilities—like her—but not werewolves—like the ultra-sexy beast flanking her. Boys were sometimes born completely canine, but generally came out shapeshifter like their daddies. The community of dogs pretty much kept to themselves, even in the Zones. As the rest of society, children were rare due to the "family tax." Reggie had heard a rumor of a pack living in the Wastelands. A pack teeming with children and the freedom to have more if they chose. Nice concept...but the Wastelands weren't an ideal place to raise a family.

The Sangs, the elegant, intelligent, sensual beasties that they were, on the other hand, were hypnotizing and beautiful. Skin like alabaster and eyes that gleamed like mirrors. They were dangerous to take as a lover. Everyone knew to sleep with a Sang was to become a Sang. If one could handle the drastic lifestyle change, being one meant being able to secure the best jobs available in the IG or Zones. Night-vision and collective high intelligence had many of them working as airship pilots. A freaking idiot's IQ climbed drastically once *turned*. There were no indigent Sangs. They were a ruling class unto themselves. Reggie nodded respectfully to one praying over his meal. "Give us this day our daily red..."

He smiled back, fangs shining in full glory. She knew their credo. She respected it. *Always stay on the good side of a Sang is my motto.* She wasn't the only hungry misfit in line. She smelled a few Zoners, and even more pungent was the sweat of the dog boys. Feral and sexy. Musky. Naughty. Thoughts of that fighter's cock down her throat, inside her, wherever he wanted to stick it, were dangerous distractions. Reggie sniggered. *A big distraction, indeed.*

The center of the room had a huge tile depiction of the labyrinth. At the dead-center of the mosaic a red-hot charcoal grill had been installed. The flames leapt up through the grating, inviting her to grill a tasty piece of flesh—species unknown. Not that it mattered. Probably goat or mutton. Maybe venison. Deer still roamed, and little herbivores had fared well over the last century.

She studied what she could of the depiction, memorizing it. Save for the grill atop it, hiding the center, it looked complete. She had a thing for mazes and puzzles. She liked them. They liked her right back too. That was where her hybrid nature took flight. She could see pathways hidden to others. They were her thing. The shortest distance between two points. The safest path through uncharted territory. She was pretty darn good at navigation. That's how she'd made it across the Wastelands without a horse or escort.

She sidled up to the line and grabbed a bowl and spoon.

The buffet was vegetarian. Mostly carbohydrates and plant-based foods. She wanted meat, but the dog boys were guarding the protein table. She felt almost too tired to fight for a scrap of meat. She looked for plant items that could be combined to make proteins. Muscle, speed and agility needed protein. Beans, rice, soy. She moved down the line, carefully filling her plate with just enough, but not too much, of things green and brown and somewhere in between. She was parched. She glanced around for a beverage service. Some half-ale would be nice.

Reggie stopped in front of an empty steamer pan whose little askew tag read "vegetable hash." She picked up the serving spoon and scraped at the remnants half-heartedly. The leavings looked, for lack of a better description, nasty. Fetid. Food shouldn't be unrecognizable and gray. The leavings of the hash reminded her of mold growing on a window screen.

A server breezed through a swinging door wearing traditional kitchen whites, his long hair pulled back by a silvery mesh. "It's been popular today," he said, resting a full tray of the hash along the tray slide and then removing the empty, which he passed quickly under the counter. Reggie assumed there was a bus tub under it on his side. The server slid the fresh tray of hash into the steamer. "May I serve you?"

Reggie had lost all interest in the actual vegetable hash and had discovered a newfound interest in the vegetable hash server. Was this unsuspecting young man her link to her trainer…or was he her trainer? "People *fighting* over the hash today?" she asked, emphasizing her words carefully.

"Visitors have been *dying* to get to it all day," he replied. "Scoop?" He held out a serving spoon of the decidedly bland-looking dish.

Reggie wrinkled her nose. "You know, I've never been a fan of food I can't readily identify." She looked up, across the protective glass covering of the buffet, into the black eyes of the server. "I'll pass on the hash."

He smiled. "Excellent choice."

"What's your name?"

"Karst."

"What are you doing later, Karst?"

"Dishes."

Reggie shook her head. "After you're off work. I'm from the Red Zone where life is tough and we fight for what we want. You're very attractive. I may want you."

Karst leaned across the glass hood. "My services are not sexual in nature. I'm assigned to the scullery. However, if you must have me, you can make a request to Fight Master Pik, though I don't think you'll have time. Welcome to the Battle

Royale, Zoner."

She withheld a yelp. "I passed? I haven't even auditioned yet."

Karst nodded. "Yes. Yes, you did."

"By refusing the dish citizens have been *dying* for all day? Tell you what, first I meet my fight master and then I'll make you the woman in a bout of coitus you'll never forget as soon as I'm given permission to do so."

He nodded. "I'll reserve myself for sodomy at your hands. I've taken a Zoner woman or two. I know it's an honor to be had by a Zoner female and live to tell the tale."

Reggie winked. "You got that right."

Karst winked back. "Eat, rest. Come back at midnight."

Reggie sauntered away with her tray and took a seat facing the buffet. She ate slowly, trying to give her empty belly a chance to re-learn the concept of "food." The Sangs and dogs were mixing it up over the half-ale.

Her repast was tasteless, and though filling, without texture.

Her dog boy had tossed a huge cut of meat onto the grate above the center fire pit. The fat spat and spattered, and the aroma was nearly orgasmic. A mantra of one long deprived of protein resounded in Reggie's mind. Her mouth watered. *I've got to get some meat!*

She left her table and approached the cold tray. The smell of raw meat made her feel heady and addled. Anxious. Primal.

The handsome shifter made a low, throaty growl as she reached for a strip of red meat marbled with delicious fat deposits. Some of his pack were in partial shift. Not quite man but more than dog. He was all man.

He shook his head. "This meat is for the pack."

Reggie picked up the meat and brought it to her nose. She took a good long sniff and then licked the bloody juices from her fingers. "This meat is for me," she said. "And if you behave, I'll share it as I did last night."

The shifter chuckled. "You like it raw and red? If that's the case, I have something you'll like." He palmed his significant bulge hidden inside a pair of simple cotton duct drawstring pants. Dogs never wore a lot of clothing.

"I'm going to consume protein now, and you're going to retract attitude, claws and dick, or you'll lose the latter," Reggie replied. *This dog boy has more human features than a wolfling. Still, he has the unmistakable scent of a were-beast, and I'm not sure which is more exciting and enticing. The raw meat in my fist or his sweet musk.*

"Meat belongs to wolves," he said through sharp canine teeth. His jawline morphed to more canine features.

"Don't get all shifty on me. I have every right to eat meat. And this piece belongs to me today." Reggie gripped the piece of steak tightly. "I'm a fighter, and fighters eat meat."

"You want to fight me?" he asked.

Reggie shook her head. "No. I want to eat meat."

"Your mouth says no, but your hands still hold the meat." He sniffed the air—a long, deep breath. "It smells delicious."

"Yes, it does. I think it may be beef."

"No...your crevice smells delicious. You want me. Your body calls to mine. You say you want the meat that's in your hand, but I think you want meat that's here." He again palmed his crotch. "We can do it now. No one will care. Make you howl, I will."

"You weren't this puerile last night, nor when you escorted me earlier, Dog Boy. Are you trying to impress the pack?"

"I'm the fighter chosen by the pack to represent us in the arena. I have nothing but their respect."

"The rest of them aren't fighting—you're the only dog boy? Good to know. Now, I'm going to eat and if Dog tries to take my meat or molest me, I'll kick ass."

The werewolf rocked to and fro on his heels. He'd shifted another step down on the evolutionary chain. Less than man. More than canine. Reggie was surprised he still had the power of human speech.

His facial features contorted, and he made his challenge. "Fight now. You win, eat meat. I win, I..." He paused, licking his chops and leering suggestively. "I eat you. Maybe you like intercourse with werewolf. Very passionate. Very dangerous." He shifted toward human again...a little. "Perhaps you desire only my manskin." He shifted to full human. "Does my beast frighten you?"

Reggie marveled at the incredible fluid nature of the dog boy. He lived in three worlds simultaneously. From moment to moment, he could be anywhere from full on wolf-dog to werewolf to wildly attractive man. Or anywhere in between.

"You're too young to mate. Your balls haven't even dropped yet." It was a terrible insult. This young beastie was in his prime. He could probably do a hundred women and still be ready for more. "I'll eat now," she continued. "And you will not stop me."

Clutching her piece of coveted protein in her strong right hand, she lashed out with her left and caught the werewolf by the throat. She pressed against his carotid artery hard and fast, cutting off the blood flow to his brain. She'd crushed an opponent's windpipe with her left hand before.

She'd caught the shifter unaware. That was to her advantage. He stumbled and fell to his knees in a spasm of coughs.

"Dog Boy finished?" She leaned forward and whispered, "Dog Boy humiliated? Will Dog Boy get pissed on tonight for being a weakling? Happens to the best of us, wolfie. We all have to take a beating to run with the pack."

He lunged upward and struck her hard across the face. Reggie hadn't been able to deflect the blow. Stunned, hungry and not in the mood to fight, she opened herself to seeing the path to victory. Her gift of sight…her edge in a fight. She couldn't see the outcome—only the progression. Always being able to see one step ahead made her a fierce opponent.

She shifted her weight and tossed the meat onto the hot grate over the fire. She bent over backward to do a back flip away from the dog, and as she brought her legs over, kicked him in the chin. He went down hard, shifting again to a more canine form as he tucked and rolled.

"You're amazing!" she exclaimed, immediately wishing she hadn't.

She stood upright and straightened her clothing. She grabbed the scruff of his neck, pulled him to his feet and held him by the throat over the grill. It took everything she had to hold him in place. He outweighed her by far. It was a good thing he was both shocked and stunned at being bested by a human female.

"Don't fuck with me, mutt. It's almost my moon time, and if I don't get some red meat into me, I'll, and this is a promise, take a bite of you from a place you'll miss the most during mating season. Do you understand?"

A larger, older shifter approached the fire pit. He had the wisdom of the ages in his eyes. This had to be the leader of the pack. "You're a fighter. Fighters eat meat." He turned and made a sweeping gesture at the onlookers. "It's an agreement between us and this lady. Lady can have meat today. Lady has earned the right."

Reggie didn't release the dog boy. He'd slipped into his manskin. She leaned forward and planted a hard kiss on his mouth and then ran her tongue across his lips. "You taste yummy, bitch." She released him, patting him on the back. "Good doggy. Now go and chase your tail. I have meat to eat." She then whispered, "It must be this way. To protect ourselves. You understand, yes?"

"I do," he whispered back. The canine shifter crept away into the shadows, shifting back into his dog form, his head low and shoulders rolled forward. Reggie knew the fate that awaited the defeated werewolf. He'd lost a fight over a piece of cheap meat with a woman. A *human* woman. He'd been humiliated. Degraded. The pack would taunt him. Probably punish him. It was their way. He'd rebound stronger and more potent in a fight. She wouldn't be able to take him down a second time. *If we meet up in the arena, he'll show me no mercy.* She shrugged. *Not that I'd want him to. We are fighters. There can be no allies. No lovers. Only victory. No matter how attracted I am to him — I may have to kill him. Before he kills me. That is the way of things. Literally…fuck my life.*

She flipped the meat with her fingers, wanting to cook it just slightly more than blue. Rare. Blood rare. She turned her head and squinted into the shadows as a painful yelp shot across the room.

Dog Boy was taking his licks. She shifted her stance, listening to the punishment coming from the shadows. *I should go over there and claim him sexually to prevent them from buggering the poor bastard. It's my right and would further enhance my status with the pack. They'd let me do it too.* But that would delay her dinner. And she was far too hungry to do a good deed. Her appetite proved more aggressive than the desire to further conquer the dog.

Her meat was rare and ready. She patted some seasonings onto it and then let it sizzle a few seconds longer. This was what distinguished humans and human hybrids from the Sangs and dogs. *We don't humiliate our weakest links by teasing and assaulting them. We simply kill them. We kill our enemy, cause intense feelings of inadequacy in his people and then rule them with an iron fist. That's the human way.*

The dog boy approached Reggie as she turned from the grill. His shadow cast a great figure across her shoulder, and she could tell by his careful steps that he was in pain. She kept her back to him, showing him who was boss.

"What would you have of me now, Dog?"

He spoke softly. Humbly. "I would speak to you, my lady."

He'd gone human in the moments since he'd left the pack in their corner. Full human. Hot, sexy, sleek. Intelligent and sensual.

Reggie turned to face him. "I'm listening." *Weakness. I must not appear weak before him. He already has me at a disadvantage. I can't want him! I may have to kill him.*

He bowed. "I accept defeat. I'm your servant. In all the donnybrooks and bouts of my life, I've never been bested so skillfully and completely by another. Not another dog, Sang or human. You're magnificent."

She knew it was a dog custom — not to be taken lightly. Either she shunned him or became a part of his extended family. "You're an admirable opponent, and I'm better for having fought you. Please, let me share my meat with you and we'll be family of flesh and blood."

The handsome male's face brightened. "I accept your offer." The flare returned to his eyes.

Reggie held up the steaming rare cut of meat and bit into it over the fire. Juices cascaded down her chin and into the coals, causing sparks and pops and a delicious perfumed steam. Still chewing, she held out the meat to the dog. He tore at it with his sharp teeth and then swallowed his piece whole.

"We're family now," he said.

"I'm Reggie Halvdan of the Red Zone. My father is Patric Halvdan, a weaver. My mother is well thought of and admired by all as a woman of justice and strength of character. She sits on the council of the Combined Zones."

The shifter bowed his head in recognition. "I'm Hundi. I was whelped outside IG's eastern gate. My sire is Sivik the Gray and his woman is Fryda of the outer circle. My mother too is a weaver. Of fishing nets. She trades them to merchants who resell them along the coastline."

Reggie bowed. "I'm honored to know your family."

Hundi held out one large hand. "We've shared meat. We're bonded. I shall not forget this day."

"Nor I." Reggie accepted his hand. "I'm honored." Hundi turned. She stopped him. "Don't go so soon. Stay here with me for a moment. I'm sorry you had to take your licks from the pack. I shouldn't have bested you in front of them. At least not in a dinner hall. Please…talk to me."

"Yes, of course. I haven't thanked you for the kiss in the alley yet—though it was to distract a peace officer, I enjoyed it. I don't mind being used now and then."

"I've carried a bit of apprehension and guilt with me since I found the Long Rider's corpse. I buried him poorly. I'm sure his body was discovered. Since I pocketed what was of value on his person—and he was an emissary of the queen—

I assumed his death would be investigated. In which case, outlanders such as myself would be queried. Fighters would be questioned. We're always questioned in such circumstances."

"He was more interested in your scar and the hiding of same than the investigation of a missing Long Rider."

"I won't hide it. It's a badge of honor to me."

"It's delicate." Hundi traced his fingertips across the web-like scar above her left eye. "It, like you, is unique, and beautiful."

Reggie felt herself flush crimson. "Oh, good god. I'm blushing. Go away, Hundi. You're much too affecting. I need to eat and get my game on."

Hundi smiled and stroked her arm. "I would have another kiss."

Reggie shook her head. "Not now."

"Later then. And if not tonight, then when we meet in the arena, I shall steal a kiss."

"Is that a threat, fighter?"

Hundi sauntered away, but looked back. "It's a promise."

His gait was strained, though regal. She felt sorry for his pain. She shook it off. He would live. He'd live to fight over scraps of meat again. There was no room for pity in the arena.

As she tore pieces of meat with her teeth, chewing thoroughly and relishing the hot, red flesh between her lips, a tall, gangly man with a deep scar across his forehead walked into the dining hall and then grabbed a bowl. He wore the telltale gray clothing of the Shadow Zone. A place of perpetual dusk and rain. Very unpleasant. It was wet all the time with little farmable land. Houses of sod and underground dwellings were unlit by the sun. A terribly unpleasant place.

The Shadower headed straight for the vegetable hash. No scoop of this, no dollop of that. He didn't even cast a wistful glance at the proteins being guarded by a new dog — one with a more wolf-like continence, who protected the meat on all fours. She could tell this new man was a fighter. His sinewy strength told her that much. Probably a Wastelander in borrowed Shadow Zone clothing. He had too much color in his cheeks for a Shadow Zone citizen. That man had spent some time in unshielded sunshine. He reminded her vaguely of an old leather saddlebag.

Reggie watched, interpreting the events playing out before her. She eyed Karst as he studied the gangly man. Server and fighter exchanged a few words. She couldn't read lips, but she could read the look of remorse in the frown lines on the server's face as he loaded a scoop of hash into the man's bowl. It was the downcast face of a man filled with pity. It portrayed two things to her, this look on his face. Firstly, he wasn't a fighter. A fighter displayed no pity. Secondly, the gangly man had already failed his audition.

The Shadower took long strides across the room and then sat with his back to a corner. He slid a protective arm around his food and lowered his head to eat. Reggie had seen this behavior before. She could probably win a money bet that he was the youngest of a dozen hungry kids. He'd learned to fight for his food and protect it if necessary. He'd make a fierce opponent. He'd been fighting to live his whole life.

Not hard enough. He had strength and stamina, but he didn't know how to use common sense. He quite obviously wasn't a good listener. She guessed Karst gave the same speech to every fool fighter who came to eat the hash. *Visitors have been dying to get to it all day.* The ability to listen closely was a skill every good fighter needed to hone.

Within three minutes of taking the first spoonful of the gray hash, the Shadower died, face first in his bowl. It wasn't a pretty sight. Death rarely proved to be a thing of beauty. Sometimes it was artful or graceful or even joyful, but never pretty.

Reggie looked hard at Karst, whose nod confirmed her suspicions. The man had failed the test.

She finished her meal. She kept alert for anything out of the ordinary. She willed her gut to hold down the food. She buried her fear.

The Sangs and a few of the older dogs descended on the dead man. One of them wore a faded emblem on his jacket. *Disposal Crew.*

Her audition had been far from what she'd expected. She'd been prepared to fight. To battle. To kill if necessary. And all she'd had to do was listen and choose wisely. She focused on the last mouthful of food, wanting to eat every last morsel, but eager to leave the dining hall of the damned.

Every Zoner was leery of eating something non-identifiable. Even when starving. Sometimes *not* eating was the way to win. In this case, the adage was true. Eat the hash, fail the audition and become Sang food. Damned messy eaters, too. No wonder there were drains in the floor and hose bibs along the walls.

CHAPTER FIVE

*N**o matter what's happening, things can always get worse. Better you look the other way and keep moving.* A Red Zone motto. She tried to remember that credo as she wandered back to her room with a full belly for the first time in days. The blood-rare meat sat like a lump in the pit of her stomach. She hoped it'd digest slowly so the fullness would continue for a while. There was nothing worse than starting a battle on an empty stomach, and although she was technically in a hotel, of sorts, she wasn't sure if there'd be another meal for her. She'd spent her life chasing meals. Devouring each one as though it were her last had become a way of life.

Reggie quickened her step. The arena…to battle her way through the labyrinth…that might be her last supper. *Either I win or die.* She was ready to win. She had too much to lose.

She whipped her long dreads around as she

skipped and punched as she walked. The little metal shards at the tips could easily put out an eye of an opponent. She jabbed the air as if in an old-fashioned boxing ring. Of course that was just an expression. The Zones didn't use rings. Fighters were dropped into pits, usually hobbled or restrained. Blindfolded. Suffering the effects of a hallucinogen. One hand strapped down. *Good times.*

Fighting was real. Tangible. Painful. And only the living could fight. Only the living could hope. Without it, you might as well crawl into bed with a pseudo—the most hopeless of all.

This was the fight of fights. The ultimate prize awaited her, and she need only speak it. To the solitary winner of a *battle labyrinthine* one undeniable request was granted.

Power? Sure. Wealth? Of course. Freedom? Most certainly. Freedom for her brother. Definitely.

Reggie hugged her stomach as she walked. Her belly churned from anguish over her brother's plight. Anguish was a weakness. *A weakness that can be used against me in the arena. The labyrinth is intuitive. It knows what a fighter fears most and uses it against you.* She'd heard it so many times it must be true.

She entered her room and secured it. An unexpected rap at the door a few moments later nearly made her jump out of her skin and into a tuck and roll. A fight or flight response mechanism. Paranoia ran deep in the Zones.

"Who is it?" The door didn't have a peephole. She placed a hand atop her racing heart and slowed her breathing.

"Your servant, lady."

She knew the voice. *Hundi.* "What do you want?"

"I must say it to your face."

Reggie opened her chamber door. "Yes?"

"Soon, you, I, and many others will cross the great gates of the arena."

Reggie yawned. "So?"

"I would make an allegiance with you, for you are sure to be a powerful ally and a frightening adversary."

Reggie shook her head. "I don't make contracts in the ring. I'm out for myself and no one else."

Hundi bowed his head slightly. "I would then ask that should we both survive to the end, you not kill me immediately, but consent to be my wife. I've heard a last wish can be granted. My kind doesn't kill our mates—even in combat situations. Thereby, I can't take your life if you consent to be my wife. You'll be victorious, and I'll die a happy man. Should we both make it out alive, I promise to share my meat with you for all time."

I bet you want to share your meat. "I'm honored, but I must refuse at this time."

She watched his face for signs of defeat. The pang of failure. He reflected only love.

"May I make a request?"

"Yes."

"I want you. Now. If we must face each other in battle in the arena, which is inevitable, I would make love to you now so when we're forced to battle each other to the death, we'll have had at least one night in each other's arms." Hundi spoke with assurance. Reggie felt both the cocksure attitude in his voice and the deep compassion cushioning it.

Handsome. Articulate. Muscular. Reggie put her hands on her hips. Already her privates grew tight at the thought of bedding the dog. *What is that old word used to express joy? Hallelujah? Well, hallelujah!*

"You're really quite eloquent when you wear your manskin," she replied, suppressing her arousal.

"My kind has the ability to be great orators, though it's hard to maintain this form. It isn't our true nature to be so human. We prefer to run on four paws and sing with the full moon."

She cast a wanton glance at his crotch. The outline of his penis strained against his thigh through the canvas-colored pants. The belt at his waist wasn't knotted. With one little tug she could have them around his ankles and that thick dick of his in her mouth. Or pussy. Or ass. Maybe all three.

"I can smell your heightened state of arousal, Reggie Halvdan of the Red Zone." Hundi leaned forward and licked his lips. "I can almost taste you."

Reggie smiled. "I don't usually do this before a fight. I find sexual frustration keeps me on my toes."

Hundi slid his arms around her waist. Reggie held her ground, blocking the entrance to her room, but allowed his embrace. He kissed her throat.

"Sexual satisfaction can awaken heightened senses, and without the distraction of a wet, wanting quim, you'll no doubt fight well." He slid his strong right hand between her thighs and pressed his fingers against her privates. "I can feel your heat. I can see it rising like steam from your desirable body."

His lips went to hers. She didn't resist. She relaxed in his arms and allowed the embrace. Their lips slightly parted, tongues gingerly exploring sensual boundaries. Shifter and hybrid kissed. It was rare that she allowed this intimate of connection—even with a lover. Kissing was a luxury item. Arousal could be taxed. Sometimes the only physical contact she had was her fist to the gut or jaw of an opponent. Months could pass without so much as a kind word. And here was a potential foe sending shivers through her from his kiss, alone. The fight or flight response rose in her gut. *I want this…I want this—but I need to get it over with. A good fighter never relaxes.*

Reggie broke the kiss and pulled the tie on his pants, which fell to the floor. She leisurely ran her fingers down his hardening shaft. "You have a lot to offer me."

"I offer all I am. Let us find love in this hour before twelve. These minutes before we might be forced to kill, let us think only of how to bring the most pleasure to the other."

Reggie dropped to her knees. "Will you pay the fee if I'm billed a pleasure charge?"

"Yes, of course."

"You may have me, but not before I have you."

Reggie put her lips around the head of his penis and stroked his shaft into her mouth.

Hundi put his hands atop her head in encouragement. He closed his eyes and allowed her hot breath and soft tongue to draw him into a state of no return. *I love you, human woman. I love you. I'm bonded to you.*

"We have the hour, my love. Allow me to enter your room and therein we shall ravish each other."

"Well, we wouldn't want to scare the other guests." She stood and pulled Hundi inside by his erection.

He slammed the door behind them. "So considerate of you to think of the well-being of the other guests," he said.

"Yeah? I've never been one to be labeled 'considerate.' Not sure I like the sound of that."

Hundi buried his face between her breasts, biting the laces of her corset. "I apologize. You're an evil bitch. Better?"

Reggie stroked his cock. "Much."

"Your touch inflames me. I won't howl. I promise."

Reggie pulled his shirt over his head. "I might."

They didn't make it to the bed. They dropped where they stood.

His full weight atop her, their mouths crushed together, Reggie struggled to free herself of her breeches. "Help me out of these things," she said against his throat. "I need you in me now."

Hundi chuckled. "You're desirous of my sex within you so soon?"

Reggie moaned. "Yes. Please."

He trailed his mouth down her body, across her bare chest and torso. His hands cupped her breasts, now freed of their constraint. He teased her dusky nipples as they hardened under his touch. As he slid his kisses down her belly, he tugged away her pants. As she lay before him she dipped two fingers between her legs. He patted them away, shaking his head.

"I shall quell your passion, my love."

He dipped his face between her legs and lapped her swollen clitoris, drawing it farther from its hood. She arched her back to welcome his oral invasion. He proceeded with long, slow tongue strokes from apex to anus, kneading her thighs and unabashedly rubbing his hardness against her leg. Reggie closed her eyes.

She trusted the dog boy. She trusted him because she'd defeated him. It allowed her to become absolutely lost to the pleasure of the moment.

He crawled atop her. She opened herself to his thick member as he stabbed at her, forcing his way into her. She came against his dick, its width stretching her, its shaft rubbing against her sensitive bud. As her orgasm peaked, he swallowed her cries with a deep kiss.

He pumped harder and faster until he had to break the kiss to express a long cry of relief as he climaxed.

"You said you wouldn't howl," she whispered, trying to catch her breath under his weight.

"So much pleasure. So much. To spill inside you was so powerful." He withdrew.

Reggie gently touched his chest. She rolled onto her side. "Hundi, did it hurt much? Your punishment from the others. Did they urinate on you? Sodomize you?"

"Dogs don't punish other dogs with pain. Dogs punish with humiliation. I was humbled and used as a woman by the sergeant of our pack. It was very brief and is now forgotten."

Reggie patted his bottom. "Are you sore?"

"Sergeant was merciless, but I'm fine."

"If I were to bugger your tight ass, I wouldn't be merciless. I'd lick you and stroke you, and when I stuck my wand into your anus, you'd come."

"You'd use me as a woman?"

"No. I'd give pleasure to Dog Boy in new ways. Would you not like to put your penis into my ass?"

"I would, yes. I'd take you over and over all night and make such friction from our love that nothing would be left but the ashes from our fire."

Reggie kissed Hundi's spine. "Well, if you catch up with me in the arena, I expect you to hold me up against the wall and bugger me until I come. And if I catch you, your ass is mine."

Hundi pulled Reggie into his arms. "I'll kill myself before I'm forced to kill you."

Reggie sighed. "That's not how the game is played."

They fell into a dead silence so thick it blanketed them as they rested in each other's arms. Reggie couldn't say the words. She didn't want to admit she had just given away strength to an opponent. She knew all the rules of engagement. Falling in love was not a means to an end. In the arena.

CHAPTER SIX

Midnight. Perhaps a few minutes after.

Reggie heard the muffled shrieks of nocturnal revelers and the whistles of pursuing authorities ten stories down. The mayhem of the night had crept into her belly as well. Her passion hidden beneath her traveler's clothing, she waited in the dining hall.

The odor of blood and bleach permeated the room. It made her want to gag. She withheld the reflex. Control meant everything.

Rank and file, a phalanx of brutes, of which she was one of three females. Represented were the Wasteland, White, Blue or Azure, Red, Fire, Forest and Eastern Zones. There were also a huge Beachling, by the smell of him, and a couple Under-dwellers. Hundi stood away from the other men. The women had moved into a group. All together, had they been mercenaries, they would have made a formidable army.

She was both seeing and being seen.

In those rare opportunities when a fighter got a look at his or her opponent, even if it was for a traditional coin toss or handshake, it was a time to gain advantage. They sized her up as she memorized all she could about them. The weapons they carried. The outline of those hidden in their clothing. And a cocked head could indicate a bad ear. Squinting could mean poor eyesight. A swift rise and fall of a chest could mean fear. So could the odor of a fighter's sweat. The way the others moved, the way they stood. The way they listened—everything could be used against them in a fight.

And this was the fight of a lifetime.

Her lifetime.

For her brother's life.

A door slid open at the far end of the room. Reggie projected her gift toward the darkened opening. She couldn't see her path. Her talent failed her so seldom. Now was not a good time to be blind.

"Are we to enter?" the Beachling asked. "There isn't enough room for more than one at a time to cross through."

"Then I guess we go in single file," Reggie replied. "Who here will go first?"

"Since you're full of answers, you go," one of the unkempt Under-dwellers said.

Reggie shrugged and took the first step through the sliding door. The others followed suit.

It opened into a long corridor. Every six feet a sealed steel door—old, locked, rusted and labeled "inoperable"—broke the monotony of the passageway. It seemed every exit was bolted shut. If she wished to change her mind, cutting out a side door wouldn't be an option.

Hundi was about six or seven fighters behind her in line. She felt his heat and sensed his gaze on the back of her head. They'd barely had time to bask in the afterglow before it was time to dress and appear as commanded.

She found it difficult not to enjoy the post-coital bliss pervading her every step. *He did me right. Satisfied isn't the word for it. I've got to shake off his touch and get some ice flowing through my veins or I'm history.* She smiled inwardly. *I have never been loved so thoroughly. In any other happenstance, I would make him mine. And have his puppies.*

She'd walked the long walk of a fighter before. Every pit, every arena, had its version of the march. The parade before sponsors, gamblers and viewers of sport. That much was no surprise. Usually, she walked alone, shoulders squared, chin up, eyes forward. Very rarely had she walked the path of champions when she could barely stand upright due to sheer exhaustion from a kiss and fondle. *Never. I've never been pummeled like this before. Hundi is a secret weapon in his own right. Why, if he did all the fighters but me beforehand, they'd be fighting in a stupor and I'd win in a heartbeat. That thought made her gut ache. Two remaining meant one winner and one more death. I don't want to kill him. I don't want him to kill me. I am so screwed. My brother's life depends upon my victory. Focus, Reggie. Focus.*

As she had so many times before while being paraded about, Reggie looked straight ahead. She stood tall and walked proudly. She wore a sash of crimson to represent the Red Zone. She had outlined her eyes in black liner, and her cheeks and lips were powdered to give her a pale, ghostly appearance.

Hundi had sat back and watched her get ready. He hadn't been able to keep his hands to himself. "I like the raccoon look, Reggie. It makes you appear fierce and mysterious."

"I am fierce. And mysterious." She'd cast a smoky look at him, her kohl pencil held out like a short dagger before her.

Then he'd tackled her and nailed her a final time. One last bout of coitus before they had to face each other in a magic arena in a fight to the death.

The line halted before a pale, thin man whose back was to an old-fashioned overhead door. End of the line.

"Fighters, welcome," he said as the steel sections of the rolling door creaked upward like fingernails across slate.

The sound repulsed Reggie. She wanted to cringe. She didn't react. *I am steel. I am solid and sharp. It will take disembowelment to break my focus. That or Hundi's mouth on mine —*

Reggie tucked away thoughts of Hundi's kisses as they were ushered through.

The little man's words carried weight, even though he was smallish. "Line up on the yellow stripe. Line up quickly!"

No one questioned his authority. They followed directions. Reggie had the feeling if this man had been boxed—his arms and legs removed—he would have continued to wield more power than, say, the big Beachling, whose body odor preceded him as they lined up.

With blinding spotlights before her, Reggie took a place along the yellow line and shielded her eyes. The light was so great she could not see beyond it. One thing was very obvious, however. The lights were not steam-generated. The heavy, moist, hot air was gone. These were pure electric, generated by some power source other than All Mighty Steam.

The guide stepped before the line of fighters. The lights at his back turned a soft pink. The tranquil light allowed for a clear visual. They were in a formal meeting room.

"Candidates, welcome," the guide began. "You answered the call of the queen, and how you made it here is your own business. The only thing that matters is victory."

Reggie withheld the urge to scoff at the speaker. *We're here because we didn't eat the damned hash.*

He continued. "I'm the royal fight master. My name is Pik. Just Pik. The name itself means 'royal fight master' in the language of the old ones. My job is to acquaint you with the rules of the arena."

Reggie spoke. "Where are we?"

"My dear girl, we're in the arena's reception hall. Once, long ago, fighters were paraded about by their communities, and wine flowed freely. Now, our sporting events are of a more serious nature. No more pomp and circumstance, you might say," Pik replied.

"When do we fight?" Reggie realized her tone sounded more than simply impatient. It sounded vicious.

"There are formalities that must be addressed.

Traditions to be honored. Are you so ready to die?" Pik asked.

Reggie turned right, then left, as she spoke, trying to catch the eye of every opponent. "I'm not here to die. None of us are. I'm here to win." She paused. "And so are they."

The fighters rumbled with agreement.

Pik smiled. "I see. I hope you meet death as passionately as you live life."

Hundi made a sweeping motion with his arms. "I'm not afraid of death. This is a waste of time. Give us our parameters, let us select our weapons from that pot of arms beyond the light and send us into the arena."

"Are you all so eager to fight?" a voice asked from the shadows.

The combatants crowed and yelped and pounded the floor. It was more a menagerie than a phalanx of trained fighters.

Pik chuckled, then bowed toward the figure in the shadows.

While the others displayed their aggression and readiness to battle, Reggie followed the outline of the veiled figure and the actions of Pik. She guessed that she was in the presence of someone rather important.

She kneeled as the elaborate garb of the figure became apparent. "My queen," she said softly. *Holy steam…this is the queen.*

The ruckus ended and dumb silence filled the hall as Queen Viktor emerged. He wore a tarnished crown and wool socks. And not much else, save for a long tube into which his penis had been inserted. Strings at the opposite end of it held it up like a grotesque erection, and even more ghastly, the mechanism stayed in place with little fish hooks threaded into his chest muscles. Dried driblets of blood snaked downward. He had a lacework of scars across the barrel of his chest.

Reggie studied the queen's appearance. *He has donned this bizarre penis gourd outfit before. Or he enjoys wearing fishhooks. The scars say that much, but his eyes are strong. He dressed like a buffoon, but he is powerful. He is our queen.*

"Combatants, I'm honored to introduce you to Queen Viktor," Pik said.

Viktor sauntered out from the half-light and into the soft glow of pink track lighting. "Welcome to the arena, fighters. You have believed in that which was said to be untrue and heeded the silent call. You're the true saviors of our society, though none will ever know the truth of it." Viktor approached the line. "Stand now, proud and true, and let your queen have a look, shall we?"

Walking much like a duck with tied feet, using very small steps much too dainty for a man of his stature, Viktor paraded before the fighters. He ran his fingers across the bare flesh and muscle of a White Zone contestant. Reggie could see gooseflesh rise on the boy's arms.

"You will note, fighters," Viktor began, "that I don't say this is my arena. My labyrinth. It isn't mine. It belongs to all of us—and we belong to it. That which lies beyond this room is the heart and soul of our world." He motioned for the White Zone boy to move a step forward. "It's the dwelling place of the spirit that keeps the checks and balances of our world, well...in check. I entered into a contract with the spirit of this place. I provide it sustenance, and it allows us to enjoy a certain amount of freedom. Without our compact, our world would once again fall into war." Viktor paused to stroke the face of the White Zone fighter. "This fair-haired, pink-skinned White Zoner shall be honored as the regent of this match. The spirit has chosen him, not I. In all things, I defer to her wisdom. Her needs. And her needs are pervasive. She's the great mother and consort of holy steam." He paused. "To this man's family a hundred sheep shall be delivered."

The White Zone boy smiled and bowed. "My queen. Thank you."

Viktor continued. "The arena isn't simply a granite and marble construct and venue for fighting. The labyrinth is a living thing. I'm its voice. The spirit of the labyrinth calls to me, instructs me and tells me what it needs. *How* it needs. It wasn't constructed, it has always been. It's the wellspring of all life and the tomb for all who have gone before us. As such, the labyrinth has needs. It must be fed. It must be healed when it founders. It must be entertained, and sometimes, it must be disciplined." He shivered as if discussing the arena caused him duress. "I realized its uniqueness as a young boy, wandering its parameter. My mother had vanished inside, and I always hoped to find her. Now, I wish I hadn't found her...*no matter.* In my youthful exuberance, I thought, wrongly, that the labyrinth usurped the strength of the people, when in fact, it keeps us all alive. After my coronation, I banned all contact sports and the various avenues of brutality for entertainment's sake in an honest attempt to save IG, the Zones and the Wastelands from what I believed was a sort of energy-sucking life force entombed in the labyrinth. I was mistaken. Oh! How I was mistaken. The labyrinth withered without the heat of society's daily battles and drama of discourse. As it failed to thrive so did Ironhedge-Ghillie. So did the Zones. It was a time of famine." He paused, obviously pained by the discourse.

Reggie watched his Adam's apple bob up and down as he held back sobs. *The queen isn't what I expected at all.*

The monstrous penis sheathe swayed as he walked. "She survives on the antisocial and brutal behaviors of the people. She feeds on our indecision, mistakes, rage and fear. I couldn't publicly reinstate the violent games of our past. That would never do, don't you see? Go from starvation to bloodshed? Not a step forward in the least. I feared war. I made a compromise that allows for a controlled environment wherein fighters such as you feed the labyrinth's beast and keep us all alive. In short, the arena is the furnace of our world. Violence and drama are its fuel. Too much, and the fire burns out of control. Too little, and we face extinction as its embers cool. The spirit of this place needs you to lift the bowl to mouth. Your little war will keep greater conflicts from happening. Fight well. Kill well. Die well, and we shall all live well. You do your world a great service this day. I salute you. And though you may never receive the admiration of our great society, in their name, I extend my thanks."

"What of the prize?" Reggie asked.

"Ah, yes. The prize. Well, there is one, to be sure. And it's tailored to meet your needs. Whatever it is your heart desires, shall be yours. There is nothing I can't make happen. Be the last standing, and the prize is yours to name."

A hushed but palpable frenzy rushed through the combatants.

The queen glanced at Pik. "They're ready, Pik. Instruct them well."

Pik nodded to his queen before turning his attention to the fighters. "The arena knows you. From the moment you answered the call, it has watched you. It knows your scent. It knows your secrets. It'll fight against you even as you fight each other. Even unto the last citizen standing, it shall deceive you. If you aren't afraid now, you will be. Whatever is in your heart shall be cast out and trod upon. Your very essence shall be poured out and pissed and defecated upon by the inhabitants of this place. They have no remorse, no code of ethics, and use our own laws against us. Be careful with whom you align yourselves, and trust no one. The soul of the labyrinth is starved. We send out the call for battle when its hunger pangs lash out at us. Until it's fed, it punishes us — it punishes our queen to hurry things along."

The queen held out his arms as if to embrace the crowd. "I'm not as eccentric as it appears. I wouldn't suffer such ridiculous attire if the arena didn't plague me day and night as its hunger grows more severe. The humiliation and pain I feel feeds the beast, but only just. I give of myself to feed the spirit of the arena until the battle begins.

It's like a great serpent, and I, the rodent dangled above its lair. The rat will satiate the serpent only for so long before it's digested and shat out, and it's time to feed again. Before the meal is offered to the serpent, it hungers and writhes in anticipation. So too does the labyrinth. I ask for no sympathy or praise, but know this—I'm the feeding tube by which the arena whets its appetite. If the call is unanswered and the battle forsaken, I will die. I'll be sucked dry of life force, and my young son will be forced to take my place. For my child's sake, and for the sake of the land and its people, the arena's hunger must be quelled. When a winner emerges, I shall again be able to don the robes of my station, for the monster shall be at rest. The more horrific the battle, the more carnage and deception and drama, the better. Use your cunning and win. Use your fists or whatever weapons you may find or carry in with you and win."

Pik nodded at Viktor. "Our queen makes a great sacrifice of his own flesh and nobility to preserve what is good in this world. Be swift so his pain will end. And hear me now, fighters…the arena has ears and eyes. Its minions roam the pathways. Its pets seek playmates and bones to gnaw upon. The fallen haunt the corridors. This is a historic site and a traditional eleven-circuit design divided into four quadrants. There are thirty-four turns. Each labyrs and lunation has its own environment. What is a lunation? It's the halo at the outer cusp of the labyrinth. The total number of them is divisible to twenty-eight—as in the twenty-eight days of a woman's cycle. The blood of life. And there will be blood, fighters. And life, for one. There are tricks and traps — many in the labyrs or spaces in between the channels, but not all perils are physical. There are many starting places, but only one true path to the center, and only one out. There is no map, no guide. The arena ebbs and flows as it extracts what it needs from you. Truly, you may carry whatever weapon you wish, though only your wits will save you. If you're injured, there is no truce or assistance. No white flag. If you pray, do so now, for the call to prayer is silenced within. It's better you make every attempt, even if you must drag yourself out, to exit. Terrible things happen to the injured and fallen. There are caretakers who see to the injured and dead, and they don't distinguish between the two. If you hesitate, and they are near, you will be rendered."

Reggie knew better than blurt out, but couldn't stop herself. "Rendered?"

Hundi reached out to stop her, to quiet her.

Pik chuckled. "Ah, I sense an alliance has already been made between combatants. Be wary of such dalliances and accords. You never know when you might be forced to kill an opponent." He paused. "And always, the spirit of the arena and the power of steam will haunt you. Now, it's my honor to initiate our regent. The regent of the arena acts like the first course of a banquet. It's a great honor to be chosen."

Very suddenly, Pik's right hand flew out and a blade concealed between his fingers sliced the jugular of the young man from the White Zone. Arterial blood spray pumped from the man's throat as he collapsed.

Reggie suppressed the jolt of shock and awe as

the swift execution put her on high alert. The thick copper odor of the boy's blood burned her nostrils.

The queen cleared his throat. "By this blood, I pledge to the victor...the lone survivor...one wish granted. No matter what it may be—even if you wish that I hang myself, it shall be done. The blood of the regent binds me to the labyrinth, and I can't go back on my word. It would know. And it would punish me. More than it punishes me now." He paused, seemingly waiting for a reaction.

Reggie didn't react. None of them did. These were fighters. Strong. Stoic.

Viktor continued, "I'd wish you good luck, fighters, but he's the lucky one. His nightmare is over. Trust no one. Everything is a lie—even the truth." He turned, his humongous codpiece whipping about. "Pik, take them to the chamber. Oh, and find out the boy's name so his family can be compensated. I do hope someone knows him. You must remind me to write down names before the blade strikes."

Pik nodded. "Their names are recorded, my queen. The wayfarer stations handle that now."

The queen, his muscular backside to the fighters, wandered away. Reggie heard him say softly, just above the final jugular pulse of the White Zoner, "Yes. Yes, thank you, Pik. Let them know I'll be watching."

CHAPTER SEVEN

Twenty fighters, seventeen male and three female, were ushered through a heavy steel door and into a ten by fifteen chamber. It reminded Reggie of a steam locomotive boxcar, though she'd never ridden in one. The box was without seam, entrance or egress, after the door locked behind them. It appeared to be one solid shell of iron, though she knew it couldn't be. Her era had no such technology. Although it could have been a leftover from the days of high technology and atomic fusion.

She found a corner to call her own. Reggie mulled over the queen's promise—and riddle. It had to be a riddle. One of the other females nodded to her. Reggie sized her up. She was a Wastelander. Had to be. Her clothing said Forest Zone, but her feral movements told another story. She probably stole the clothes. Is there any sense in making an ally at this point? If push comes to shove, I'll kill her. She cast her gaze to Hundi. No matter how much she wanted him inside her again, she'd kill him too. Freedom for her brother was worth more than any single ally or lover.

The shore-dweller—the large, foul-smelling Beachling—spoke first. He stretched his powerful-looking arms out before him and yawned. "Is this where we're to rest before the battle begins?"

An Azure Zoner spat on the blemish-free shiny metal floor. "Blue needs no rest. I say the battle is now!"

The Beachling rushed the Azure. "So be it!" He thrust his body like a juggernaut and the Blue Zoner struck the wall, which clanged like a bell but didn't dent. "I can kill you now with my bare hands!" He clutched the Azure's throat. "I'll rip out your throat and use your blood as war paint!"

Reggie pressed deeper into her corner—crouched, ready to spring into action. She had a vantage point where she could see all her enemies and their reactions to the pending slaughter of the Azure Zoner. She studied their body language and eye movements as the Zoner's throat split open and the shore-dweller snapped his head off with one motion. No one flinched. No one trembled. These were worthy fighters, indeed.

The bloodied Beachling kicked the Azure's body aside and spread his palms against the cold wall. The handprints he left made a poor memorial marker.

"Who's next? Who'll take on Malik of the Eastern Seaboard?" He turned to the Wastelander female. "Will you, girl? I've fought females before, and the cunning of your sex makes you a worthy opponent. You try to deceive now, do you not? Your clothing says you're a forest dweller, but you're clearly a Wastelander. You look hungry."

The Wastelander shook her head. "I can't defeat you confined as we are. I may be a Wastelander in borrowed clothing, but I'm not a fool. If you let me live until you've killed all the others, I'll let you have me now. However you want it. It's a fair trade."

Malik raised his bloody hand and striped his face with the Blue Zoner's blood. "Whore."

"No, sir. I'm a virgin. I ran away from an arranged marriage and chose to enter the labyrinth for a chance to gain my freedom from our tribe's traditions," she replied. "Women of my clan are deflowered by their father's choice of husband as a part of a ceremony, then they're passed from man to man in both clans until all have used them. Her brothers, uncles—even her father—and sometimes women of the clan have at the bride. It's a cruel custom. Especially when the bride is very young. I've seen women's spirits shattered by such treatment, not to mention the physical trauma they've endured. If a girl refuses the suit of her clan, she'll be staked out to starve to death."

"I see why you came here, but can you fight?" Reggie asked, surprised.

The girl nodded. "I've been fighting all my life. From hunger, fists and the ruinations of man, I've fought. I'm quick and strong." She turned her gaze to Malik. "And pure. My brothers have killed men so that I remain pure. Will you accept my offer, Malik of the Eastern Seaboard?"

"How do I know you haven't poisoned your

womanhood?" he asked. "Wastelander women do such things. I've heard it to be so."

"Is not trust, on some level, a part of every accord?" she replied. "I assure you, my vagina is not slicked with poison, but the need of a woman desirous of an accord."

Malik laughed. "Indeed. You're a scrawny wench but comely. I'll taste your virgin's blood against my lips, and I promise I'll kill you last." He approached the young woman as he unfastened his trousers.

His penis was already at full mast. He had a penile piercing. A pointed barb through his foreskin. Reggie shuddered. That will hurt. Maybe that was the point.

Devoid of modesty, and obviously able to achieve tremendous potency in desperate times, he pressed his large body against the girl's, smothering her against the wall.

He looked over his shoulder. "If any of you disturbs me in any way, I'll pull out of this woman, rip off your head and fuck your skull."

A nervous hush closed the walls in further. No one was going to interrupt the compact between Beachling and Wastelander.

Reggie wanted to look away. She knew better. Never take your gaze off your enemy. It bothered her—this fleshy agreement, though it wasn't the worst she'd witnessed. This isn't the most desperate situation I've been in. The needless bloodshed of the Zoner, this public sex act, locked in a boxcar, about to fight to the death. This is foreplay.

A tendril of desire crept through her at the very

sight she abhorred, but she dared not even glance at Hundi. She could take him—right then—with the fighters watching and the virgin's blood flowing, but that would be a mistake.

Malik had torn away the Wastelander's undergarments and had poised his huge cock to strike home. The Wastelander had no control. He easily carried her slight frame in his arms. He kissed her.

Surprising, that. Odd. Tenderness in the embrace of the Beachling—though he was about to rip open the hymen of a virgin with a barbed dick—was unexpected. Reggie saw a glimmer of pleasure in the girl's countenance as Malik at least tried to arouse her before harpooning her to the wall.

Malik slid one large hand between his conquest's legs, and in the dead silence of the boxcar, the sound of her readiness became apparent. The Beachling stroked her mound, and the sounds of wetness against his rough fingertips told a story of ardor and desperation.

It was during a kiss he entered her. She cried out into his mouth. He held her fast and locked his lips against hers as he beat his hips against the wall and his dick in and out of her.

Reggie's sex twitched at the squish of coitus coming from the torn quim of the Wastelander, pummeled by the ample dick of the Beachling. Was the sound from blood or female nectar? She wanted to believe it was the woman's body readying her for orgasm. Every virgin should achieve climax. Even in those conditions.

Malik pulled his mouth from the girl's face. She

had a red ring around her lips and a glazed look in her eyes. He arched his shoulders back and roared as he exploded.

Reggie wanted to press out an orgasm of her own as a long moan escaped the girl's lips and she trembled with pleasure. Yes, she had achieved orgasm. The Wastelander would die last if Malik defeated everyone, and she wouldn't die a virgin.

Malik let the girl slide down the wall onto the floor after dragging his hand against her bloody thighs. She smiled weakly. "I thank you, sir. Please, protect me a moment longer while I recover. I'm spent by your embrace."

Malik turned and took a protective stance before the girl as she rested. He ran his fingertips across his lips, smearing her blood along his chin. "Sweet," he whispered. "Sweet like the first kelp of spring."

He hadn't tucked away his member. His semen dripped blue. Blue like the sea and tipped with white foam-like caps upon waves. I like blue. It's a nice color. Malik might be a decent lover under any other circumstances. Oh, I shouldn't think that way. Hundi wouldn't like—

Reggie chastised herself for her familiar thoughts toward Hundi. They weren't betrothed or otherwise tied. They'd had sex, that's all. I can think about other men if I so choose! She glanced at Hundi. His eyes were smiling at her, and she could see the outline of a slight bulge in his pants. He wiggled his fingers at her as if to say "Hello."

No…I won't think of other men. For now. After I kill him, I'll move on. Until then, he's my lover. The dog wearing a man's skin is my lover. Though he may be more, someday. If we survive. Crestfallen, she withheld a long sigh. There are no survivors. Only a single victor.

Malik eventually sauntered back to his original location in the steel box, a look of pride on his face accompanied by an unmistakable smile. The woman pressed herself into the wall, which had only minutes before acted as the bed of her defloration.

The third woman, a desert dweller, spoke up. "Malik…"

"Yes, desert woman?" Malik said.

"Was she a virgin?" the desert woman asked.

"I broke her barrier. I felt it pop and her shudder in pain as I entered her. Why?"

The desert woman shook her head gently. "You've taken her maidenhead, and now, according to the customs of her people and yours, if I'm not mistaken, you're married. Thereby, it's forbidden for you to kill her. First or last, she can't be killed by your hand. I've heard the laws of our various societies apply to the arena."

"I've never followed the rules. Why should I start now?" Malik asked.

The Wastelander laughed. "Because I'm now your wife, as these witnesses can attest. The labyrinth knows everything about us, Malik. It shall know I'm your wife and that you can do me no harm."

Malik arched his head and growled. "You tricked me!"

"Better trick you than be the first to die. At least now I know I have a chance of survival—with you out of the equation." She gestured at her additional opponents. "Not to say these citizens are less suited to win this battle than I. I mean no insult. I'm just saying you're the biggest, the strongest, the angriest, and now, you're no longer a threat. At least to me."

Reggie smiled. "Brilliant!"

The Wastelander bowed. "I may be half-starved and from a region where a rabbit pelt is more valuable than another child, but I'm not stupid. I saw the Beachling and knew what I must do. Of course, the fact that I knew he'd take me well and fully—and without hesitation—also played a part in my decision. I saw him looking at me earlier, and I used his coveting of my body as a weapon."

"You're a true fighter." Reggie placed her hand on her heart and bowed. "I salute you."

"I shall capture you, and when I'm finished with you, you shall wish for death so strongly you take your own life," Malik said. "And you, Red Zone fighter…you'll die slowly. I promise you."

He's afraid, Reggie thought. The labyrinth was already working against the fighters. He fears defeat more than any of us. "I'm not afraid of you." Reggie yawned. Her eyelids grew heavy. She gasped. The air was off. Smelled off. It had a purplish tint. "We're being gassed," she said, seeing others drop to the floor. She looked at Hundi. He'd vomited and had passed out. She joined him in a fitful sleep a moment later.

CHAPTER EIGHT

Reggie awoke alone.

A curved wall stretched out before her on either side. A wall comprised of perfectly precise blocks. Hundreds of thousands of them. Granite? No…marble. Smooth, perfect, highly-polished marble. The slabs were each about three feet square, and she could see no mortar. She ran her fingers along the slight indentation separating them. The space between stones was too small for even the tip of a knife to enter.

The ground upon which she sat was a combination of gravel and hard clay. Hard as rock, really. She scratched it with her nails. *Terra firma.* Barely a trace came away.

From her seated position, her back against the wall, she studied the marvel of engineering. There was no ceiling. What appeared to be an endless night sky spanned out before her, and below that, walls of around twenty feet in height stretched out as far as she could see. Midpoint along the walls, every six feet or so, were sconces radiating electric light. Their hum was the only sound to break the stillness other than the heavy breaths she took to clear her mind of the effects of the purplish gas. She was lightheaded and sick to her stomach.

Reggie pulled herself to her feet, fighting the urge to vomit. She took a few steps, checking the ground under her for the telltale signs of a traveler. Footprints? None. Disturbed gravel? Some. She sniffed the air. Yes…her body odor lingered in the crescent-shaped corridor. The odds were already against her. She looked left. *There is one way in and one way out.* There was no variance, no landmark. Everything looked the same. She couldn't even scuff the ground to leave a mark.

Time to utilize my hybrid gift. I hope it works here. She opened herself to seeing the most promising pathway. There was no glimmer along the path. Perhaps her talent couldn't be utilized in the arena. Reggie scoffed. *Of course it can be used. I refuse to believe it can't.*

She exhaled slowly and scanned the labyrinth again.

The road glowed before her. Just a slight shimmer. A path had been revealed.

A failing skill and nineteen enemies. Well, eighteen and Hundi, who could slay me with his kiss alone. Though I hope for more. Maybe in our next lifetime.

She took stock of supplies in her pack and weaponry. *A canteen and a pouch of salt. A small knife. A Wastelander gas mask. A length of rope. The metal shards woven into my hair.* She chuckled. *My foul mouth, vagina, and fists. And that's about all I've got to work with. I'm sure I could find a way to use my eyeliner as a weapon, but I think I can leave it under "personal items" at this point.*

She took her first steps, hugging the stone wall. It was warm, like fireplace bricks. She crept along slowly, quietly. To the right. Traditionally all subsequent ones should be taken to the left. Common knowledge. A labyrinth had form and meter. Maybe even this one. This wasn't a maze. It was a true labyrinth. One way in, the same way out. Salvation in the center. For some. To some.

She picked up speed, hoping to get her first battle over with. A left turn appeared. The heat of the wall she followed with her hand grew in intensity.

Reggie looked carefully at the apex of the turn for shadow or reflection. She sniffed the air. A pang of need wrenched her gut as the olfactory act of sniffing reminded her of Hundi. *Where is he?*

She listened with stern focus for some break in the dead silence. *I must proceed. The idea isn't to avoid the others, it's to defeat them. Without being killed in the process.*

She unsheathed her knife and held it out as she would a mirror, hoping it might echo whatever lurked beyond the turn. The switchback led to an entirely different environment. Reggie moved carefully around the bend. She found herself surrounded by thick, curling, writhing foliage. A thousand sinewy fibers emerged from the glass-like obsidian-black walls. The light of the first corridor vanished.

She stayed dead center, calling upon her hybrid vision to guide her. She couldn't see the path, but she could see through the camouflage of the walls. The vines weren't merely set decoration. The vegetation was the walls. The glassy reflection was their nectar. They were ravenous. Sweet-smelling, siren's song walls.

Reggie gritted her teeth and crept carefully along the damp trail, over slime and ooze. The ground was like a sponge. The vines rattled as she passed. Their perfume tickled her nose. She stayed just out of reach. The walls secreted an enticing scent. It smelled heavenly. It could so easily trick someone weaker. Someone without her hybrid abilities. Someone who lived by his nose. A dog boy. *Holy steam, I hope Hundi doesn't fall into the hungry maw of this carnivorous plant structure.*

She gasped as the faint glow of a mage-light appeared. It gave off a weak light. Its owner had to be dead or dying. There was just enough of the fading life-light to show her the vegetation along the walls would soon be sated. Two fighters — both from the Eastern Zone by their clothing — had been pulled into the tendrils and were slowly being consumed. A horrific chorus of carnivore and flesh assaulted her. The slurp, slurp of the vines and the crack of bones as marrow was consumed sickened her. *I want that light.*

The mage-light — a glimmer orb much like an animal familiar, common to those in the east — flickered as she moved silently by the horrifying scene. The fighter whose life force fed the light reached out for assistance. His jaw had been eaten away. He couldn't call for help. His comrade was already dead, his innards spilled into the hungry tendrils.

Reggie's stomach turned. *There's nothing I can do to help. All I can do is end his suffering. His staff lies at his feet. If I'm quick enough, I can grab it and deal a fatal blow to his skull.*

She dropped to her knees in the slime and extended her right hand to take up the staff. "I'll help you die honorably." The man's eyes closed. Shaking and bloodied, he reached for his mage-light and moved it closer. She retrieved the staff and used it to slide the light even closer. "Thank you for this."

An aggressive root pushed out the man's left eye.

Reggie stood, took a breath and made careful aim.

She swung hard and her blow landed true. The man's head split. His chest rose and fell for the last time. She picked up the mage-light, which immediately tuned to her personal frequency. It fitted in her palm, but she preferred to let it grasp hold of her corset so she could keep the staff in both hands, at the ready. Now that it'd adapted to her aura, the little light would stay with her like a pet. A very useful object, indeed.

To which god do those of the Eastern Zone pray? She should say something, even if while moving away from the bodies now shrouded and enveloped by the carnivorous plant life. *Gods of energy, fire, water, steam, give these fighters strength in their next life. Men from the east are honorable warriors so treat them as such.* It wasn't much, but it was better than nothing.

The sticky residue on her knees had seeped through her breeches and chilled her legs to the bone. She thought of the warm wall of her starting place and wished for its clean heat instead of the mossy, swampy ground cover preceding her. The cold slime seemingly penetrated her blood flow. Her nipples hardened and her fingers grew numb. Her teeth chattered.

She hastened her pace, eager to find the next bend and get away. Away from the carnage. Away from her first kill of the battle.

She'd killed before. She'd killed to end the suffering of another in more than one battle. That was the fighter's way. An old scar on her belly ached as her mind fought a flood of emotions long suppressed. Each scar meant victory. Each victory meant life. Each kill meant she'd live one more moment.

The ground beneath her shifted from mud to soil and then hard-packed clay the closer she came to what she assumed was the next bend. The endless night above remained unchanged.

There was a definite change in the wall not too far ahead. She wished she could tell where she was. *Not knowing where I started makes it difficult to discern how far I've come. Where are the others? Where is Hundi? Does he live?*

A few steps farther along, a foul odor of burning oil assaulted her, and the unmistakable glow of fire filled the twilight of the corridor. She had that makeshift gas mask in her pack. It was half-assed at best, but better than nothing. She slipped it across her face to help filter the nasty, burning stink. Tar-filled smoke wafted out from around the corner as she drew closer to the bend. Huge, looming figures cast shadows on the wall as they swayed by their fire. Reggie forced her inner path to the surface.

Show me the way, she commanded. *Show me the way.* She prepared for battle, her new staff out before her, ready to smash and pulverize.

Her vision arrived on a crimson fog. Humorously, she saw herself trapped between a rock and a hard place. Not so humorously, she quickly interpreted the symbolism. *I can't press on in this direction, nor can I turn back. This path has no length. No width. No future.*

She held her breath, every muscle tense. *Go back? Fight? Flee?* She set her gaze upon the walls of the corridor. Was there another path? *Yes…up, but I'm here to fight. Avoidance isn't my path.*

She stepped into the glow and crept carefully around the corner.

Reggie couldn't tell if the two beings dancing before a small cauldron of flaming oil were human or hybrids or something in between. They looked wrong. Just plain wrong. Deformed couldn't even describe them. Mangled? Mutated? Mutilated? Mauled?

The switchback of the turn was in shambles. A block had been pried loose and had crashed to the ground. The interior, one of ten labyrs—open spaces between the turns—lay exposed.

The greasy little creatures looked as surprised as she was at the encounter.

They didn't charge her. They didn't take a combative stance. They merely stopped dancing, still holding their arms up and hands in mudra-like positions.

They spoke to each other. "Look, a fighter has come to us. A fighter of fine caliber. A fighter who has not yet suffered the degradations of the arena," the first said to the second.

Reggie couldn't tell if they were male or female. "You aren't of the twenty sent into the arena." Her muffled voice sounded as if she'd swallowed gravel.

The creatures twittered. The first exhaled and said in a cloyingly sweet singsong voice, "That we certainly are not. We're the caretakers of this place. We dispose of the remains of battle. Take off your mask that we may see your pretty face, fighter."

The other spoke up. "We cook the flesh and bones and leavings of combat into oil and polish, polish, polish the pathways and intersections. The songs of past slayers live on by our hands. If you listen, you can hear them."

"I'll leave you to your duties," Reggie said. Pressing her tongue hard against the roof of her mouth, swallowing her fear, she stepped sideways between the flames of the beasties' cook fire and their motionless, pensive forms.

She made it to the other side—the reverse side of the caretakers. Their backsides were hollow. She watched in horror as the creatures literally turned their skins inside and out again so their faces were where their open back cavity once had been.

"Alas, maiden warrior," the first said.

It was interrupted by the second in mocking tone. "She is no maiden. I can smell her quim. It has been well-loved."

The first waved the other away. "Alas, warrior, we can't allow you to continue *your* duties."

"I'm here to fight, nothing more. Since there are bones still strewn about this place, should you not allow me to leave so you can continue your job? I shall be on my way. Should I fall, please allow me to join the songs of the fallen, but not before that time, if it comes," Reggie said.

"What is it you saw with your hybrid vision, fighter? Most fighters avoid our smoke and flame and run the other way. So many are brave only when light shines upon them and cowards in the dark. The last who ran away from us met death in the open mouth of the large carnivorous plant that guards this turn. And here you stand before us, seeking safe passage. Surely you must know we can't allow that."

Reggie saw no reason to lie. "I know my path." She studied the shadowed interior of the labyrs just beyond the creatures. *Curious enclosure. This is a dark place. A place I shan't travel alone. Not by choice, anyway.*

"You're fortunate to know your path," a caretaker said. "You must surely know that to enter into the break in the wall would be detrimental to your health. Travel into the heart of the arena is dangerous. Bad things await you in the dark. Worse things than you can imagine."

"I'm very good. And I'm not afraid. Tell me more about the regions within the walls. What revenants of the past haunt them?"

"The only thing inside the labyrs is bitter death. It's better you remain with us. Do you have anything that requires polishing?"

Reggie wrinkled her nose as one of the caretakers offered her a dirty rag saturated with the oil of fighters long dead. "I take it the death you offer is less acrid, hmm? I'll be on my way now."

The closest caretaker reached for her. "As you

have surmised, good fighter, we do not suffer the living well. Perhaps you'd fall against your own knife so we can render your bones and flesh without having to deal with the abomination of your life force. And don't think you can escape by darting around us and into the labyrs. More gruesome horrors lie therein. Have we not made that abundantly clear?"

Reggie took a step away.

The second caretaker took one closer. "We shall have to dispatch you. We can't allow you to depart us yet able to draw breath."

Like a sheet caught in the wind, the beastie flew at Reggie, enveloping her in the foul-smelling caul of its hollow, fluid body.

Reggie's arms were trapped, though she still held the staff. She spun around on her heels and caught the second caretaker with a hard blow. It flew back and landed without a sound. As the suffocating, mucus-like shroud spread upward to her chin, under her mask and over her lips, Reggie caught the cauldron on the end of her staff with another turn of her heels. Though she knew she might be burned, she tilted the staff end up and the pot rode the wood to her trapped hands. The boiling liquid splashed across the front of her body.

There was a shriek. A loud, long, horrific, banshee-like shriek. Reggie wasn't sure if she'd made the sound as the oil burned her hands and legs, or if it was the gelatinous caretaker's death throes that inspired it to fill the labyrinth with a sound akin to an eagle shrieking across the sky as it dipped to grasp its prey. Perhaps the shriek was of two voices.

There was searing pain. Nothing short of death could ease the force of it as it cascaded from nerve ending to nerve ending, shattering her concentration, breaking her will and sucking breath from her body. Everything around her went black. *So this is it...I'm dying.* She dropped to her knees, only vaguely aware that her arms and legs were free. The odor of her own charred flesh assaulted her.

I'm dead. She crossed the shadowed threshold of lifelessness and the pain subsided. Only the memory remained. She cringed at the thought. *What horror to have died with that as my last memory.*

* * * *

There was no light or welcome by deceased loved ones at the end of a tunnel. There was only restless blackness. Blackness like a drop of ink in the sun. A rainbow of colors so dense and well-mixed they formed the darkest of hues. Her body flexed in waves of time as her death rolled her spirit out to sea.

She didn't expect to awaken. In the steam gardens of heaven or in hell. Eternal sleep was it. One long nap called Death.

CHAPTER NINE

Hundi felt Reggie's spirit leave her body as if he stood right next to her and was witness to her soul's flight. He smelled death. Her death. He shuddered and silenced a wail of grief. He stopped his heart for a moment. Stopped breathing. He could feel his veins run cold. There was no warmth without her.

He shifted completely canine in form. A large, gray wolf-dog. Feet the size of dinner plates and keen, sharp senses. It was his fastest form. He tasted the air and followed the scent. If she were dead, he would stand by her body. They had mated. Even in death, he would protect her.

Nothing mattered but the scent he followed. Not the sweet, enticing odor of flowers or the caustic stink of burning oil. Through all the scents of the arena only hers mattered. Her flesh sang to him.

He found her.

Burned, dying. Beautiful still.

* * * *

"There, there, my beloved. You must rest."

Reggie heard the words, but couldn't grasp their meaning. *Rest? Beloved?* She fought through the fog of pain to whisper, "I'm alive?"

"You're alive," the voice replied.

"I can't be. I battled the caretakers. They…" she whispered through a throat sore from sucking down hot fumes.

"One dead, one gone. Strange, hollow little beasts. I believe you quite surprised them. Never once have I heard a tale where they encountered the living and the living survived to tell the story."

Reggie opened one eye. "Hundi?"

"It is I."

She reached out with a bandaged hand. "My knife…"

"No need to kill me just now. We can wait until you're feeling better."

"I was dead."

Hundi chuckled. "No, you were burned and unconscious. Funny thing, that."

Reggie opened her other eye and turned to face Hundi, who lay beside her. "Funny?"

"Yes. Truly. The bedtime stories of the caretakers make sense now. Their oil isn't intended for use by the living. It's the essence of the dead, and it's used to keep the labyrinth sated and well-groomed. Though in this case, my love, you have been doused with holy oil."

"What? I was dead. I felt death. I crossed the line between this life and the next. I recognized it. I've been there before and made the journey back."

"If you were dead, then before I carried you to

safety, you were resurrected. You've been anointed and blessed, and I've lived to see a childhood wish come to pass. The oil that burned you was created from the bones and flesh of a thousand heroes. I thought it was another myth of the arena, but now I see that it's true. You were burned and dying—perhaps you were dead—but the flesh that has remarkably returned to your frame is endowed with the will and grit of those who went before you. I've seen and heard their stories as you heal. The knitted flesh of your left hand told me an epic tale. And your belly, your lovely belly, told its story in a sonnet. Marvelous!"

"You're a lunatic, Hundi. You're marveling at things that can't be true. Flesh doesn't sing."

"Look at your hands, my love. Do you not recall the burning of your skin from your bone? Do you not recall the smell? It was that very scent that drew me to your aid."

Hundi held up one of Reggie's hands. She squinted and trembled at the touch of his against hers. It caused her pain and arousal—a combination she had, at times, felt quite agreeable. Like now.

"My hands were gone. No flesh. Charred bone," she said, marveling at the baby-bottom smooth skin covering her fingers and palm. A whisper caught her attention. "What did you say, Hundi?"

"I said nothing. It's your flesh. The flesh of heroes. They sing. Tales of love and war and conflict and resolution. Of their fields at home and the airship shadows over their crops."

"Are they going to help me win? If they don't intend to assist me, then they can shut up."

"That, my love, is a song shared only between you and your flesh and bone."

"Where are we, Hundi?"

Hundi stroked her forehead. "We're hidden. I prayed to holy steam to let you live as I masked the scent of your charred flesh and carried you to safety."

Reggie breathed a sigh of relief. "Thank you, Hundi. How are we hidden?" She rolled her face into his palm. "I'm so tired. Please tell me we don't have to fight to the death, at least not now. I feel safe with you."

"You are safe with me. This isn't the time for us to cross blades, for we aren't in the arena but above it. Thereby, please don't roll too far left or right."

"We're atop the wall?" Reggie asked.

"I carried you here like a she-wolf might carry her pups to higher ground. We're high and away from the others. They haven't yet perceived that the labyrinth has fighting surfaces in every direction. Did you know there are portions of this monstrosity that are without gravity? I should very much like to battle in that section. It was my starting point, and let me tell you, I was quite taken aback to find myself midair upon awakening. The others…they don't engage their senses. They don't perceive the nature of the arena."

Reggie tried to sit up. "Can we walk the length? See the way to the center?"

Hundi nodded. "I'm sure we could, but that isn't the purpose of our journey now, is it? We must battle. We must win. We can't avoid conflict and expect to have our dreams come true. For now, however, you must rest."

Reggie snuggled into his arms. "Thank you for protecting me, Hundi. Shift fully, if you must. I know your human form is cumbersome. I…I am grateful for you. For the warmth you've given me in this cold place. For the hope of a better future, though I know that is not my lot."

"I shall change soon enough. I'd endure my manskin for all time if it'd keep me by your side. It is better for me to solve the riddle of this place wherein only one can exit alive. I must find a way for us both to leave."

Reggie closed her eyes. "I'd like that, Hundi. It is odd that there is a low tone wafting about me now. I am my own musical instrument. My arms prickle and whisper of the queen's dilemma. Of how he's tortured by the spirit of this place, but that he brings much of his pain upon himself. He isn't a well man, Hundi." She paused. "Tell me, after I wake up, will you make love to me? I find I missed your touch during our separation. Though our time together has been short and furious, and we are not guaranteed happy reunion outside this arena, I feel as though you are the only constant I have. Not my fists, not my determination. You."

Hundi growled seductively and fluidly shifted from man to gray wolf. He curled up against her.

Not opening her eyes, Reggie reached out and patted his back. "Good dog boy."

CHAPTER TEN

She heard their songs.

Their voices were a chorus of dramas, tragedies and comedies. How many centuries, even before the war, had the labyrinth demanded the aggression of the citizens as sustenance? There were too many…too many voices for the time that had passed. The songs of her flesh caused vivid visualizations that catapulted her dreams into far-flung realms. There were miraculous things lost in the past. The choir now sharing her body stood witness to past glories.

They believed she was one of them. A fallen hero turned waxy paste, living on as mortar and polish in the heart of the world.

"I am alive," she called. "My battle continues."

Always, the replies came in rhyme. "She who draws breath, take careful step. Victory then, shall you intercept."

"Yes," Reggie replied.

* * * *

Reggie awoke to Hundi's kiss. "You were uneasy as you slept. Let me comfort you." He nuzzled her throat and pulled away the cloak he'd used to wrap her.

She returned his embrace. She pulled his face to hers and entwined her fingers in his thick, yellow hair. She felt his hard male body against her new skin. The warmth of his torso against hers created a cascade of shivers across her belly and up her spine. It wasn't long before she put her legs around his and he was inside her.

He thrust slowly at first, building strength with each pass of his hips. She could sense his wariness. "I'm well enough for this and more, Hundi. Please, take me as you wish." She dug her nails into his hips and pulled him inward. "Take me."

Hundi hastened his pace, entering her deeply. Buried inside her as far as he could go, they climaxed together. Quietly. Discreetly. Reggie bit her lip as she quaked. Never had trying to be quiet been so difficult.

As they lay entwined atop the smooth stone surface of the labyrinth, quiet all around them and not so much as a flicker of light, save for the glow of the sconces from below, a very soft, very light voice echoed. Reggie wrapped herself around Hundi. It felt secure. Safe. Right.

"My flesh sings," she whispered. "I think someone liked our little romp. Do the heroes not know that when mid-battle one shouldn't draw attention?"

"Your ribcage is the culprit, I believe," Hundi said. "Shall I silence the heroes of your flesh or just ask them to sing very, very quietly?"

"Will they listen?"

"I doubt it. Fighters are an arrogant lot."

Reggie stretched her arms around his neck. "Yes. Yes, we are." She paused for a moment, basking in the sweet sweat of Hundi's body. "Do the stories say how long the fallen heroes shall rest within me?"

"I hope I'm around to find out, for this legend is being written with each breath."

"Ours is a tenuous relationship. I may have to kill you before this is over. Puts a damper on things, doesn't it?"

"That I may have to kill you causes me great consternation. It's so much easier when I shuffle off this mortal form and go canine. Tomorrow doesn't matter. Only the here and now. It's the human in me who wishes victory. The dog just wants to run free."

Reggie ran a hand along his smooth chest. "Here and now can be just as complicated."

"Are you well enough to proceed?"

"I think so. The others are far ahead of us by now." She paused, considering the situation. "That could be to our advantage. Maybe they've killed each other off."

"I'm sure some of them are dead. I heard the cries of the wounded and roars of the victorious as you slept. From up here, so much is clear," Hundi said. "I saw an open wall leading to the nether regions of the arena when I took you from the caretaker's flames."

"Yes. I saw that too."

"Dare we investigate? Perhaps therein is a path with an element of surprise."

Reggie nodded. "Up here, we've removed ourselves from the fight. We can hear and see without the fog of battle blinding us. Inside the walls, we may miss opportunities." She cast about for something to wear. "I need some clothing. Mine is no doubt in tatters."

She moved about her perch. She stretched her legs and arms and watched Hundi rifle through their pile of belongings.

"I saved what I could. Your breeches are oil-stained but not badly burned. Your corset is destroyed, as well as your tunic. Your boots are intact. Your knife and staff have been scorched but are usable. I'm afraid your cosmetics are completely melted." He passed her a bundle of clothing. "However, I saved your light. What a find, beloved. Taken off one of your kills?"

"It was a mercy killing. The man was already dying." She took her breeches from Hundi. "Thank you. Will my pants sing since they're stained with the oil of fallen heroes?" She held them up and spoke into the seat of her pants. "Hello! Please promise me you won't break into song while I relieve myself!" She turned to him. "How embarrassing would that be?"

He laughed, but quickly silenced himself. "The legends say nothing of fabric. I hope you find some comfort in that."

Reggie dressed quickly. "I can see I'm not fully healed, but I'm in no pain and, in fact, feel quite frosty. Combative. Feisty." She scanned the horizon. As far as she could see was labyrinth. She turned slowly, trying to get a directional feel. "I can't say which direction leads to the center."

"I think it doesn't matter which way we travel. Either here or below, we must follow the curve of the wall while we take out anything in our path. We'll reach the center one way or another."

Reggie sheathed her knife. "And then we have to make our way out."

Hundi nodded. "One of us. Alone."

"Presuming the final battle will be fought not in the corridors but in the eye, that is. I won't hesitate should we meet up with another fighter before we reach the center. I'll do what I must." Reggie took his arm. "Come on, Dog Boy, let's get a move on."

Hundi smiled and shifted gracefully into full canine form.

Reggie stroked under his chin. "Lead away, my friend. I can keep up. Even with a wolf-dog."

* * * *

She felt the change in her companion as he raised his snout to sniff the air. "What's going on?"

She almost fell over from the push of energy in Hundi's wake as he ran from her side. Reggie righted herself and caught up to him in no time. She patted his back. He growled, low and deep.

"What is it?" Reggie asked softly, not wanting to disturb the vast silence too greatly.

Hundi pawed the capstone upon which they traveled. Twice.

"Two fighters are near?" Reggie circled around, looking for anything moving. "Can you tell who they are?" She unsheathed her knife. "I can't jump down fifteen feet and expect to walk away unharmed. Even if I timed it perfectly and landed atop them, I'm going to get hurt. I'm not ready for that again so soon."

Hundi padded around in a circle as if creating a bed from tall grasses. He growled, "Under-dwellers." It sounded rugged and thick coming from canine vocal cords. His thick, gray mane bristled and he panted, tasting the air. With one solid motion, he head-butted Reggie, knocking her off her feet, and then turned on a dime and leaped off the precipice. She fell back, landing hard on her backside. She couldn't stop Hundi's attack. She scrambled to the edge and peered over the side.

He'd landed atop a slightly built, but surely stealthy, Under-dweller. Of the two he was the smaller target.

Under-dwellers didn't have a homeland. They lived within the boundaries of every zone, on the fringe. In the shadows. They were of a caste even lower than common Wastelander. They died like any other citizen, however.

Blood covered the passageway. Arced sprays of red. Abstract art of the most gruesome kind.

Hundi seemed to ignore the arterial spray and bit deeper into the throat of the smaller fighter. With powerful jaws and muscles like steel, he used the man's body as a weapon against the other.

He struck the second in the chest and sent him hard against the wall. Gray matter mixed with blood as the man exhaled a final breath.

Reggie called down, "They didn't fight. Why did they not fight?"

Hundi shifted to full human. "They didn't see or hear death's approach. Their blood is befouled by opiates. They were oblivious. I believe the old term is *stoned*."

She stood erect and clutched her blade, touching it to her heart. "Fallen ones, I salute you." Though the dead were doped and hadn't died well, she felt a pang of remorse at their loss. *Fighters who numb their minds and bodies with drugs are truly sad*. She re-sheathed her blade. "So few ease life's journey by drugs any longer. I've heard stories about Wastelanders who make potions from roots—not to defray pain in a battle or stave off hunger—but to induce a dream-like state for pleasure. I don't get it. Why would anyone let their guard down by becoming intoxicated, especially here?"

Hundi spat blood and cleared his throat. "Under-dwellers are unclean. To taint one's blood is a coward's path through a battle."

"Your nose is very keen. I wouldn't have detected them until it was too late," Reggie replied. "Can you catch me? I want to do more than just observe from above. It's time to fight. It's time to win."

Hundi nodded. "Most assuredly I can, beloved. Trust me."

Reggie wasn't sure if she should dive head first or leap feet first. She chose the latter. Hundi seemed poised to catch her, and if ever there was a time for trust, it was now. She sent their belongings down before her and then sprang off the edge.

There was no time to panic. No time to tuck her

knees. Before she could pull in a breath, she was in Hundi's arms. "You did it," she said, relieved.

"Did you doubt me?"

"Put me down, please."

"I'll steal a kiss first."

"The mouth you offer for kisses is the same one that moments ago took the life of a fighter. It's his blood that perfumes your lips. I'm rarely lost for words and have always taken what I want when I find it, but now, Hundi, do I embrace you out of respect for the dead or as a reward for your prowess in a fight?"

"You're over-thinking the situation. Kiss me because you want to kiss me and for no other reason. We're fighters. We've seen death. Caused death. Defeated death. This is who we are, and our kisses are just as sweet as those shared by lovers under a tree in the moonlight. If we're to enjoy each other—even in this place—we must move beyond conventions and preconceived notions of what is right and what isn't."

Reggie nodded. "I'll kiss you."

Hundi held her head to his in a long, deep embrace.

She found it difficult not to lose herself in his arms. His kiss fired her belly and made her pulse race. The flavor of fresh kills on his lips heightened her senses, and the aroma of coppery blood and a powerful man's needs overwhelmed the luxurious, romantic moment.

Her feet touched the ground as their mouths parted.

"You arouse me," Hundi whispered. "The heat of battle and taste of blood are nothing compared to the fire I feel for you. Here." He patted his chest. "And here." He palmed his groin.

"I said if we should meet up in the arena your ass would be mine," Reggie replied, stroking his cock through his trousers. "Now isn't the time."

"Shall we see what there is to claim as spoils from the Under-dwellers? There's a quiver and bow." He retrieved a small crossbow and quiver of arrows from inside the cloak of the man whose head had cracked against the wall. He stood thoughtfully for a moment, staring at the blood streaks. "Well, this is an odd turn of events," Hundi said.

"What are you talking about?"

"This is truly a wondrous place. Or perhaps it's the tainted blood I ingested affecting me. In the reflection of this fighter's wet blood upon these polished walls, I see stairs."

"Stairs? What stairs?"

Hundi spat. "My head is clear. I'm not compromised. And I do see steps. Turn, beloved. You stand with your back to them."

Reggie turned and gasped. "The labyrinth is itself a fighter. This is a trick. Vines that consume flesh and stairs leading into solid walls of stone — it's a trick."

Hundi dropped to his knees to rifle through the pockets of the fallen. "Or our salvation. If it's a trick, let us diffuse it. I won't step upon them until I see the results of the action. I need something to simulate the weight of a foot. A stone inside a boot, something like that. I won't step forward until…"

"What about the smaller one's shoe stuffed inside the larger one's boot?"

"Yes. That will suffice." Hundi removed a right boot and right shoe from the fallen fighters. He stuffed the shoe inside the boot. "Perhaps I should bite off a foot at the ankle. If I'm to simulate the weight of a footfall, why not use a real one?"

Encouraging him, Reggie made a throwing motion with her hand. "I'm not sure it will matter. Go ahead…toss the boot."

Hundi flung it at the first semi-transparent, once-invisible step.

It landed on its side.

The step grew opaque and shimmered.

The boot disappeared.

Reggie gripped her staff as if an enemy blocked her path. "Attach a rope to a second boot, and if it disappears, pull it back. I want to see where it has been."

"And how will you do that?" Hundi asked, tying off a second boot to a long strand of cord from the waist of the man whose blood splattered the wall.

Reggie wasn't ready to divulge her talent. Not yet. "Trust me."

Hundi cast the second boot onto the step. It vanished instantly. He pulled on the cord. "I can feel its weight."

"Pull it back." The boot returned through the mysterious portal. "Well, that's interesting," Reggie noted.

Hundi gripped her forearm, turning her. "I sensed hybrid qualities in you. You're truly amazing, my love."

"I have hybrid sight. Give me the boot." She opened her eyes to the nature of the boot's path.

She clung to the cord, tying it off, and tossed it out before her. "Oh, my," she whispered. "This boot went a very long way in a very short time, indeed."

"How far and well can you see?"

"I see pathways. Around corners. Sometimes the images are foggy and I can't interpret them. Sometimes, as with this boot, the journey is clear."

Hundi slid one arm around her waist. "Where did it travel?"

"Its path extends from your fingertips to the farthest reaches of the arena. Dark places where no fighter treads. Inside the walls. I'm sure of it. That place, Hundi, we shouldn't explore. It isn't our route."

"No matter where you begin in a labyrinth, there is only one path to the center and one to the exit. There can be no places in this arena that haven't been walked upon by a fighter. Even the darkest of places have once been kissed by candlelight."

"I see the path to darkness. I see the heart of this place, and it isn't at the center."

"What would happen if we traveled the path of the boot? If we took the steps to darkness?" Hundi asked.

"I don't know."

"What path do you see for us?"

Reggie nodded to her left. "We need to follow the one at our back. My sight is comfortable with that direction. I sense nothing but a long dark path through this unseen passage. My flesh crawls at the thought. It isn't fear that prickles the flesh I share with the songs of the heroes. It's a sensation beyond fear."

"Your second sight is truly enhanced by the songs of your flesh. You could make your way to the center and out again without meeting or fighting another soul, couldn't you?"

Reggie allowed herself to be pulled into his arms. "Yes, probably, but that's not why we're here."

"Let's away."

CHAPTER ELEVEN

Reggie walked with the dog, one hand on his back, the other on her staff. She'd slung the bow and quiver over her shoulder. The mage-light clung to the strap of the quiver, casting a gentle glow. Hundi's huge tri-blue eyes shone like beacons against the dim light of the corridor.

The walls took on a transparent sheen as the light touched them. Reggie felt eyes upon her back and turned. The bodies of the Under-dwellers and the mysterious portal were lost in the shadows. She knew they weren't more than twenty feet away, yet darkness had swallowed everything in their wake.

"We're in a long channel. This means we've crossed deeper into the labyrinth, if I understand how such things work. This is good. We grow closer to the eye."

Hundi growled.

"Yes, my friend. I know others walk softly in the dark with us. Their weapons are not drawn, for I haven't heard the sound of metal against brass rivets or the swoosh of blade from sheathe." She kneeled and whispered into Hundi's pointed ear. "They're just ahead of us, no? Just beyond my magic light."

Hundi pawed the flagstone ground. His immense pads stirred the dust, which hung in the static air like a gag.

Reggie stood and armed her crossbow. "Step into the light or the place I shoot may be more painful than death itself."

"Red Zoner, your threat doesn't alarm me. I smell blood. Fresh blood. Are you the victor or the wounded?" a voice called from the shadows.

Reggie fired an arrow into the darkness. It penetrated its target. A deep gasp and the sound of the steel tip penetrating fabric and flesh rang through the stillness. "If my aim toward your voice was true, you're now dead or dying, and that's all that matters."

"Boastful bitch!" A juggernaut of sheer force plowed into Reggie, sweeping her away from Hundi's protective stance. She rolled backward, an enemy upon her. One blow after another she stumbled from feet to backside. She picked herself up and fought back against powerful, unearthly powerful, fists. She deflected and aimed. She jabbed and kicked.

In the darkness Hundi yelped. She envisioned his throat being slit.

The blurred image of the fighter continued to pummel her. A hand went to her throat. A blistering hot hand.

As oxygen failed to reach her lungs and brain,

and the morphia-like long sleep of death closed in on her, one final thought rested in her heart. *My death comes at the hands of a Fire Zone fighter. Magical bastards.*

She lost her footing and fell back hard. Onto nothing. Into nothing.

CHAPTER TWELVE

For the second time since entering the arena, Reggie awakened after not expecting to return to life.

Her throat felt raw, and when she examined her injury, painful little blisters popped and bled their clear liquid. She couldn't take a full breath. Not that she wanted to. Powerfully foul air...air that hadn't felt movement or witnessed the glow of a candle or danced upon any breeze for a hundred years surrounded her.

She had awakened in a dark place.

Here was a place long overlooked with dust so thick that with the glow of her mage-light, she could count the layers like rings on a tree. It seemed completely undisturbed save for a single irregular imprint. *The boot. That Fire Zoner tossed me into the vortex.*

A single cloud of dust rose as she moved. It tickled her nose.

As disoriented as she was, it soon grew worse. Her arms and legs felt like lead and her breathing became labored.

She caught a flick of dust on her tongue. It had a bitter, astringent flavor. Her mouth puckered. She was certain it was some kind of paralytic agent. *This isn't just dust.* Gingerly, she pulled herself to her feet and walked, as lightly as possible, across the poisonous silt.

The environment was hell and removed from the arena proper. The darkness turned to dusk, and the dust grew finer and finer the farther she stepped away from her landing point until the smooth black glass ground of this portion of the labyrinth became clear and clean. Beautiful, actually. She could see her reflection.

Each labored breath stabbed her. *Broken ribs.* She held her side and moved on. "Hundi? Hundi, are you there?" she whispered. Even a soft voice echoed. *What does that tell me? An echo means I'm in a large enclosed area filled with various shapes from which sound can vibrate and rebound. There was no echo in my previous corridors.* "Hundi!" Her own voice returned to her. It stabbed her. I must continue. I must find him—though I am alone in this dark place.

Alone had always been good. Before. Before she'd entered the arena. Even the trek across the Wastelands alone was easier than being alone there. In the twilight of the labyrinth. Without Dog Boy.

Reggie scoffed. *I've grown too dependent upon him. He isn't my personal guard. He's another fighter with whom I've been sharing body parts. That's all.* "That's all!" An errant tear trickled down her cheek. She wiped it away. *Holy steam…bring us together again.*

Her words echoed back to her, wrapping her in emotion. The chorus seemed to go on forever, reverberating around unseen silent witnesses making up the place.

"That's all what?" a heavily-accented voice said from the shadows.

"Who's there?" She didn't have her staff or bow and quiver—only her small knife. Other than the poison behind her, what could she use as a weapon? Her wits. "Your accent…you're from the Wasteland Islands, far north of any other zone."

"Originally, yes," the voice replied.

"There are no islanders in this fight. Why are you here?" Reggie took a defensive posture, squinting through the dim light to try to make out the size of her opponent. Islanders had a poorer diet than most. That made for smaller men and bulky women.

"I'm such as you."

"How do I get back?"

"Why would you want to do that? Am I not pleasant company?" the voice asked.

"I left my companion rather abruptly. He'll be worried."

The voice chuckled. "One less to kill is what I think that dog boy you call friend will think. One less throat to nip. Tell me, fighter, whose idea was it to toss the boot?"

Reggie acted surprised. "Boot?"

"The boot you allowed to pass through the portal from where you were, to where we are now."

"Step out where I can see you," Reggie

demanded.

"If I step out, you'll undoubtedly try to kill me. Let me assure you...that would be difficult. Not with the poison cast about this region of the labyrinth, or your knife, or your delicious carnal nature can you slay me. I can smell your passion, strength, and yes, even your fear."

"I've heard the voice of boastful men many times. You posture now, friend. There is fear behind your words too. All beings die. I've killed obviously lesser men than you. Hear me now. You don't kill me, I won't kill you. I want to move on. Do you know the way?"

"I would have done so years ago had I found an answer to that question." He paused. "Am I measuring time in years still? Oh my. *Deshflee aghatnee.*"

Reggie changed her stance. "*Deshflee aghatnee.* What's that mean? It sounds like gibberish."

"It's the language of my people. The Islanders," he replied. "*Deshflee aghatnee* is a phrase congruent with your words for...well, let's just say it means I should be counting my time here in decades, not years, and how silly of me to forget that."

"How is it you're alive?"

"I've never once said I'm alive. In fact, I'm not."

"You're a Sang."

"I'm a Sang."

"I don't intend to be your next meal," Reggie whispered.

"I didn't say I was hungry, did I?" the Sang replied.

Reggie waved the mage-light before her. "What do you want from me? Say it now or let me pass."

"Put the flicker orb away and I shall impart my sad tale to you. You're injured. I can help."

"I'm not dousing the light. Tell me from the shadows." Reggie paused. "What's your name?"

"I'm Graham. I was Graham. No one has called me by my name for generations."

Reggie wasn't about to let her guard down. "Graham, why are you here?"

"I'm like your boot. I was cast aside."

"Were you a fighter?"

"I walked this labyrinth long before the games of the new queen came to pass. I walked this labyrinth before the war. I walked the labyrinth when steam was just hot water and electronics ruled the world. Fighter, I have a fairly comfortable abode not too far from here. Will you sit with me? It has been a long time since I've had any real social discourse."

"I'd just like to move on," Reggie replied.

"To where? To see whom? Dear fighter, there is nothing else for you once you pass through the portal. *This is it* — the bright center of your universe. We're in the place of forgotten souls where light never glows above dusk, and where death would simply be a break in the monotony. I suppose for you, the fight continues, but I, personally, have seen no evidence that the game continues for me. This is it. Truly."

"Oh, I'm getting back into the game. I'm here to fight. This is just another opponent." Reggie dramatically waved her free hand. "The labyrinth is an obstacle to be met and conquered."

"You aren't tethered to your point of deployment, and as such, you'll most certainly not land in the same place. You could land in a lake of fire or into the open maw of a carnivorous plant. I assume your advent into this dark heart of the labyrinth was accidental. An unfortunate accident," Graham said. "Or were you too cast aside?"

"Cast aside like an old boot, eh?" Reggie asked.

"I was a victim of betrayal. I was forcefully introduced to the Sanguinarian society, and as I experienced that first surge of immortality, I fought my attacker. It was a brilliant attempt on my part to put asunder my maker with my last iota of humanity. Alas, I won, but I fell in whole to this place. And that's the tragedy of my tale."

Reggie relaxed her knife hand and called herself back to attention. "You were turned and came here before you…"

"Had a chance to feed, yes. I killed my maker and have never experienced the burning lust my contemporaries call the *blood passion*. I've never said the prayer of the Sang. I'm no longer human, but because I've never refilled my own veins with the life force of another, I'm not truly a Sang, either. I'm nowhere. Living nowhere."

"You don't have the heat vision or sonar hearing of a Sang? How have you survived?"

"I'm dead. There's no need for me to survive. I simply exist. Now, I do have some creature comforts in this forgotten zone. There are other portals in the world, and some citizens use them to get rid of their trash. The things I've collected over the years! I have amassed quite a collection of forbidden items, and have also managed to keep abreast of current times by taking the time to read the crier notes dropped down every now and then.

You're the first human to pass my way in a very, very long time. Come with me, fighter. I promise you'll be unharmed and unmolested." Graham paused. "I see the fear of rape and murder in your eyes, and I must assure you that I don't find sexual satisfaction in acts of violence, nor, as attractive as you are, are you my type. When I had a choice, I preferred males."

Reggie couldn't help but laugh. "You're an undead homosexual?"

"With a once fabulous fashion sense. I'm sure I'd be a very popular upper class groomer if I wasn't trapped here. I bet even Queen Viktor would use my services."

"He could definitely use assistance in his choice of attire. When he addressed the fighters he wore a tube-like codpiece affixed to his chest with hooks and not much else."

"He has pierced flesh?" Graham asked. "And sports a penis gourd?"

"Yes." Reggie dropped her knife hand to her side.

"How wickedly marvelous."

She took a more relaxed stance. "He says he's controlled by the spirit of this place, though in the same breath he states he placates her by feeding her just so much...but never quite enough to keep the arena from sucking us all into the vortex of hell. Theirs is not a healthy relationship."

"She is a harsh mistress. And assuredly, she is in control. Any power Viktor believes he has over the arena is an illusion or fantasy given to him to help keep him pacified. I know her better than most, for I've been her plaything longer than any others. The duality of her nature is harsh. Steam is hot, fierce, powerful, and unforgiving. Steam's consort is patient. Very patient. Combined they create a being that prolongs the torture of others. I'm not sure if that was the plan, but that's the truth. Tell me, fighter, are you thirsty? I have a bottle of wine from the old era. Would you like a drink? And I can tell you, the labyrinth is, without a doubt, a controlling bitch. A bloodthirsty, controlling bitch. And coming from me, who could so easily be a bloodsucker too — that's saying a lot."

Reggie nodded. "I would very much like a drink, but I don't want to be your beverage of choice."

He laughed. "Lovely! Follow me." He stepped from the shadows, a hand extended in friendship. "I won't take blood from you. If I do, I'll want more, and the wanting will do me in as there is no satisfaction to be found in this place. I'm not so terribly miserable that I wish to end my half-life existence."

Reggie found herself unable to withhold a gasp of amazement. "Goodness, you are beautiful." She immediately wished she hadn't reacted so strongly to the very handsome white-blond man before her.

"Yes, I'm a pretty boy. Alas, my good looks are useless here. The labyrinth is all woman and isn't interested in playing doctor with a man who would rather play house with another man. Still, I think she retains hopes that she'll convert me from time to time. I know she enters my dreams to seduce me. I suppose she wants me to become so sexually frustrated I give in to her desires and make love to a wall or something. I've dreamed of children coming from such a union. Labyrinth born. Can you imagine it?"

"Have you ever been with a woman?"

"Yes, but it ended badly. Come along now…my comfortable niche isn't too far."

Reggie followed Graham along the dim path. As they rounded a corner, the walls on either side were stacked with items she presumed had been tossed into a vortex. She'd never seen such a collection of old televisions, computer monitors, and the ilk of history past.

"I had no idea the arena was so diverse. I thought I'd be tossed into a fray and have to fight my way to the center and then back out again. I wasn't sure what to expect, but never in my wildest imaginings did I believe it was a rubbish tip."

"If you're still fighting, the labyrinth has a plan for you. It needs to feed, and it will do whatever it must when Viktor gives it the chance. And funny…Viktor thinks the diet plan was his idea. The arena feeds in many different ways. Neglect just makes her stronger." Graham stopped and pushed a large wooden plank with his hip. "Home sweet home." He slipped in past it and motioned for Reggie to follow.

The first thing she noticed…bags of the poison dust. "You're the one who poisoned the portal."

Graham pointed at a driftwood and bone chair. "Sit. And yes. Every now and then something alive and very angry appears. Hybrid cats are especially difficult to tame. One would think a little pussy would love to have a lap to sit on and a scratch behind the ears, but, no…they'd rather disembowel a person. Hissy little creatures. So I poison them before my eyes can be scratched out."

"This is amazingly nice for being trapped in a forgotten portion of a labyrinth. Do you know where we are exactly?" Reggie asked. Graham did have a nice setup. He had all the comforts of home, but what comfort did the undead really need? "How much of this stuff do you use?" She picked up an electronic tablet device, its guts hanging out like spiders legs. "This resembles a scrawl-pad."

"It's the great grandfather of the scrawl-pad. I dissected it and found nothing of value in its circuitry. I do enjoy a good tinker here and there. Before I was made, before I took that fateful stroll into the labyrinth, thinking I was going to get sex, mind you, I fixed things. It was before the war, you know. I was pretty good at repairing things like dishwashers and stereo systems."

"I've heard the words, but I've never seen either. They were operated by electricity," Reggie said.

"Electricity is heaven-sent, and once this fascination with steam ends, I'm sure we'll all get wired up again. I can certainly see worshipping a hot, steamy god, but really…praying to water vapor has never been my style."

"Do you have a map of this place?"

Graham handed her a glass of wine. It smelled sweet and had a rich amber color. "Drink up, friend. This stuff is one hundred and fifty years old."

Reggie never accepted a drink she hadn't poured herself. She watched carefully as Graham poured himself a glass from the same bottle. He lifted it in a mock toast and downed the contents.

"You'll see, it isn't poisoned."

She nodded slightly and lifted the glass to her lips. "So, do you have a map?"

Graham pulled up an old wooden crate and sat across from her. "I do."

"I started at a corridor of white blocks. Roughly hewn. I followed it and it turned into a brackish environ of flesh and bone-eating plants. After that, I came upon two caretakers, who wanted me to kill myself so they could boil my remains." Reggie took a very small taste of the wine.

"You were placed in the far east quadrant. We're in the northern most inside reaches of the labyrinth," Graham replied. "Each circle has a set of caretakers. They brew the oil that keeps this place strong. The flesh of heroes, you know. The corpses of those you fight and kill will become holy oil."

"Hundi rescued me from becoming body butter. He took me up top to recover. It's an entirely different world fifteen feet up."

Graham motioned with his glass for Reggie to drink. "There is something you don't know about the upper level. There are barriers. You can't see them until you're atop one, and by then, it's too late. You'll become trapped. And then you'll die and rot. It makes the caretakers crazy. They cannot retrieve the bones of the fallen when they are encased between two barriers."

"You've pursued this line of escape?"

"It's easy enough to climb to the top of the wall. And for several hundred yards one can walk freely and unmolested. In any direction, just beyond the safe zone, however, is a barrier. An impassible obstruction that can't be seen, only felt. I spent at least two years, maybe longer, exploring the invisible wall hand by hand by hand. It's solid. It seemed to have no height or width restriction. You know, at one point, all fighters were dropped into the same area of the arena. The battle was over in minutes. The game is keeping you apart for as long as possible before the final, and inevitable, bloodbath."

Reggie didn't react to this new information, even though she found it titillating. *I mustn't fall victim to his stories. The more he speaks, the more I find myself lulled by the voice of a Sang. Sirens…the lot of them. I need to win so I can save my brother. And maybe see Hundi one last time. If he lives.*

"Can I see the map?"

"On the wall, behind that piece of red fabric. I haven't decided what to do with it yet, really," Graham replied.

Reggie rose. "The map?"

"No, the fabric."

Reggie lifted the soft crimson veil hiding Graham's map. "We are here." She pointed at a location directly below dead center. "You have it marked."

"I believe so, yes. I sometimes hear voices on the other side of the wall. Fighters or caretakers…I don't know which. All I know is they can't hear me, nor do they cross over the embankment. I've marked portals with little yellow dots. The objects that arrive have an aura about them, and if I study said object, I can see its origin."

"There are yellow dots outside the arena's parameter. Does this mean you're able to discern between objects sent into the vortex from the outside as opposed to those, like me and the boot, which arrived from within?" Reggie turned to face Graham.

"I can, yes."

"So, logically, if I can find a portal, or vortex, as Hundi called it, I could end up outside the arena."

Graham nodded. "Or back here. Or somewhere more unpleasant. Somewhere very unpleasant."

"Why can I not re-enter the portal to get back into the fight?"

"*Or somewhere more unpleasant* are key words in this conversation, my dear. You don't know where you'll end up," Graham replied. "Drink your drink."

"Where I'll end up isn't important, because I know where I've been. If anything looks familiar when I emerge, I'll have an advantage to traversing the climate." Her still-healing skin twitched. She rubbed her arm, trying to calm it.

"The arena is full of traps and perils. You could emerge in a pit of molten tar or a steam tunnel. Your flesh will be burned from the bone. Or you could emerge in a region without breathable air," Graham said. "It really depends upon *her* mood. She's a haughty bitch, she is."

"Or I could emerge ahead of the others and be ready for them when they pass. Please, I must have this map, and I must go through your portal and rejoin the fight."

"Your wish must be great. What is it? Love? Health? Wealth?"

"Freedom," Reggie replied.

"Ah yes. Freedom. The most tantalizing goal of them all."

Reggie pulled the map from the wall. Her flesh hummed. *I need to leave this place. The fallen heroes urge me forward. I'm not safe here.*

"Don't do that. The map is mine," Graham said. "What is that humming noise? Are you purring?"

"No, I'm not, but I'm returning to the portal, and I'm taking this map with me. Is there nothing I can do for you that will suffice as payment? If you wish, I'll find a way to return for you. To free you too."

"She'll never let me go."

"Who? The labyrinth?"

"I'm her toy, her midnight snack, her unwilling companion of dubious consent. My unending suffering nourishes her between battles. As long as I suffer, she'll always have the upper hand. She'll be very, very angry at us if you go through the portal. You must be a part of her plan or you wouldn't be here."

"Come with me," Reggie said.

"'I'm too comfortable in my cage,' said the little trapped bird."

"I'm not afraid, Graham. You shouldn't be either. The worst that could happen for me is death. Death is just another battle, and I'm a fighter. And you can most certainly be punished no more painfully than how you've been for the past century."

"You don't know her. From queen to me, her undead plaything, she demands a certain behavior," Graham replied. "No, I can't follow you. I'm too weak. I'm her bitch."

"You don't belong here. You're a Sang! Sang are airship pilots and run the justice system. You need to be with your own kind."

Graham slumped into the chair Reggie had vacated. "Sang are disposals and disposable."

"Come with me, Graham. You haven't yet lived the full life of your kind. Together we can escape this place. Graham." Reggie paused. "I'm going through the portal."

He cast a wistful look about his belongings. "I've worked very hard to make a good home for myself here."

"This isn't a home. It's an arena." The tingling in her arm grew stronger. The hum became more pronounced.

"Forgive me, but do you keep another sentient familiar, besides your mage-light, up your sleeve? Your arm is singing," Graham said.

"I fought the caretakers. Their oil splashed upon me. I should have died. I was badly burned. Hundi rescued me and took care of me while I healed. He says I've been anointed with the oil of heroes, and their songs will live in me forever."

Graham dropped to his knees. "No wonder she directed you here. You're a banquet in your own right. *She* must want you desperately. I now find myself wanting to consume you. I admit that. I want to taste your blood and marrow. I want to get lost in the maleness coursing through your veins. I thought it was your chosen profession that gave you such a strong aura of masculinity, but it's all you. For they are a part of you. How delightful. Let me taste them, please. It has been such a long time since I kissed the flesh of a man."

"Not gonna happen, Graham. If you come with me now, I'll allow you use of my body. You can hold the flesh of the heroes, and I shall offer a cup of my blood to you, but you may not turn me. The cut shall be mine. The control shall be mine. I'll give of myself to help you enter Sang society strong and able."

"It isn't you I wish to hold. It's the ensemble of heroes within you. There have been so many…so many. I felt their presence. I feel them as their song grows stronger. Some came so close to this place I could taste their sweat on my tongue. I pounded my member against the wall until I climaxed, hoping they'd feel my need and find a way to cross over."

"I'll put a bag over my head, bind my breasts and let you take me from behind. Anything! Let's get out of here. The heroes sing of danger. They sing of dark places, and their tune isn't a happy one. They wish us to leave. Now."

"You'll voluntarily make me whole?"

Reggie tried to take a deep breath, but found herself unable to fill her lungs. She forced a breath and vigorously exhaled it. "Yes, but only if you move—now! The pressure of this place is suffocating me. I can't breathe. I need to get away!"

Graham took Reggie by the arm and dragged her from his shanty in the dark. The portal wasn't far. The way seemed to narrow before her. She winced as the burn and sting of sharp edges ripped her skin, and all around her the clang and clunk of falling metal assaulted her sense of security. The place was closing in around them. *She* was angry, after all.

The poison dust had been disturbed by the quake of the arena's wrath. Graham pressed on, while Reggie had to cover her mouth and nose. The dry powder seeped into her pores, making her muscles ache and her skin smolder. The songs of her flesh grew more pronounced. An urgency spurred her on, and she knew it didn't spring from her gut but from the bellies of the heroes she now carried within.

Graham clutched her arm in desperation. He pulled her through the cloud of debris. He had amazing strength. Much more than he should have had for a non-fed Sang. His grip hurt, and he moved with skill and purpose. He swung around once and looked at her. His eyes were bloodshot and his skin had grown tight around his face. It was the face of a Sang about to feed.

Before she could stop herself from flying against the stone wall, he pushed her into it. She smacked her head hard and then everything went black.

CHAPTER THIRTEEN

She awakened in a pool of blood, and immediately hoped it wasn't hers.

She knew it was.

She lay face down. Her legs were spread.

Reggie rolled over and stood. She pulled up her breeches, and through the dimness she saw Graham. He stood against the wall, his head back and face covered with drool and blood. His trousers were open at the fly.

She gathered her wits and channeled her energies into her strong right fist. She met the jaw of her attacker. Almost as if he were made of paper and feathers, he flew up and hit the ground behind them.

The twinge of heat from the bite of a Sang jolted her. It came from her inner thigh. "You son of a bitch!" she yelled. "You bit me! You bit my thigh. And you used me—used the flesh of the heroes while I was unconscious. How could you do those things when I offered myself to you to save your freaking life? Graham, answer me! Answer me now!"

"I tasted your blood when you hit your head going through the portal. I felt so strong. Such exuberance I've never known. I needed more. I couldn't help myself. I closed my eyes and imagined you were a young man of my city. Fair-haired and tanned. I simply completed our transaction. No need to be so angry."

"You sick fu—"

"Cursing at me won't change the situation. My spittle now mixes with your blood, and your blood nourishes the flesh of the heroes. My song will be sung, and Graham of the Islands shall not be forgotten. If a child shall come of our union, the Mother will be pleased with me. It'll be the first labyrinth-born. A child of the arena, a child neither alive nor dead and yet a part of both worlds. A child of life and death. The first of a new ruling class."

"You shouldn't have done those things, Graham. You didn't have my permission." Reggie moved only her eyes as she surveyed the exit through which they'd passed. *I'm technically weaponless. The shards in my hair. My belt buckle.* The stiff leather belt still looped across her waist, and the thin, sharp edge of the buckle would make a fine weapon with the right hand to wield it.

He licked his lips. "I couldn't help myself. Your blood…it empowered me. And it's not as if you were a virgin. Get over it."

"I was ready to help you," Reggie said.

"And now?"

Reggie began a slow striptease, starting with her belt. Holding the buckle in her right hand, she used her left to open her shirt. "You're right, Graham. I'm not a virgin. I like sex. I've always liked sex."

"Are you offering yourself to me again?" He sounded hopeful.

Reggie leaned forward, straddling Graham. "Don't get up. I'm going to give something to you, all right."

"Oh yes. Please."

"I like sex, Graham. I abhor rape. I won't tolerate any man, living or dead, taking unlawful liberties with my body. You took my blood. You used me as if I'm some kind of glory hole." She slashed the sharp edge of her buckle across his throat. "Not twice is all I have to say."

He reacted defensively, his hands going to his neck. Reggie scowled into his panicked face as he tried to staunch the flow of blood from the wound on his throat. She slashed again. His head teetered. She stood upright and came down with juggernaut force, and slashed one final time.

"No one takes me without my permission."

Reggie squatted over Graham's nearly decapitated body and braced his forehead with her strong left hand. With her right she continued cutting. She severed his spine and tore his head away.

She held it aloft for a second and then tossed it aside.

Reggie backed away and then sank against the opposite wall, breathless. Tears flowed. She let them come freely. She'd killed using her bare hands before. She'd killed because that was what fighters did. She wiped Graham's blood against the wall.

"I'm a fighter."

She touched her mage-light. Its soft glow doubled the light of the passage. It was then she noticed the other bodies. At least a dozen scattered about the corridor. Some were twisted and contorted. Some had been hacked to bits. Others had the telltale sign of strangulation.

She knew their faces.

Through her tears, she took a quick count. Two dead in the carnivorous plants. Two dead at Hundi's hands. She cast about, almost frantically. *Is he amongst the dead?* She sighed, relieved. *He isn't. He lives. At least, if he's dead, he isn't lying with these rotting corpses. Me, him, the four dead. And one death in the box. There are sixteen here. Who killed sixteen? There are only two more besides myself and maybe Hundi. The newlyweds. The Beachling and the Wastelander.*

As clear as if it were her father sitting next to her at supper, the voice of a hero rose. "A hook to pull and coals so hot will see these fighters fail to rot. Caretakers come to toil and boil, flee now or forever become one with their oil."

Reggie shook her head. "I don't think I can stand bad rhymes for the rest of my life. However, the message is well taken. Which way?" She hoped her hybrid sight would lead her away from the carnage. Alas, the shimmering path lay through the bodies.

At least my sight is strong here. She progressed slowly. With caution. Her body ached, and her head felt swollen and sore. She reeked of Sang, and she could almost feel the displeasure of the labyrinth at the death of her toy emanating from the walls. It scratched like an angry cat.

None of that mattered.

The circling path became smaller and smaller. She was near the center.

The squishy sound of her steps in muck and the coppery smell of Graham's blood sickened her.

Graham used me. He took my blood. He deserved to die. Her thoughts lingered on the moment she'd heard his neck snap. It was a pitiful death for a blood-drunk Sang. He should have waited. He should have controlled himself. *I would have helped him find a state of exaltation, not demise.*

The song guiding her stopped. *Am I on my own now? Have the heroes deserted me?*

The encouraging songs of her flesh were replaced by the sound of despair. Sobs. Sobs lingering in the air like tiny bells.

A heavy salt spray assaulted her. The air was thick with it, as if she'd reached an ocean at the end of a desert. Her heartbeat was too fast for her to calm it. She could see the opening just ahead.

Dead center. There she knew she'd fight and win, or fight and die.

The scent of wet dog reached her. She recognized it immediately.

Hundi had arrived at the center too. She closed her eyes and breathed in the scent of her dog boy. How comforting. *He lives. He is here. My love…my opponent.*

She stopped just outside the entrance to the center, staying in the half-lit shadows.

"I smell you, Zoner! Enter if you dare!"

Reggie knew the voice. It was the Beachling. *What do I know of the Beachling? How can I meet him in battle? He keeps his word, though he's an aggressive brute. He has a sense of honor.*

"Beachling, are we the last?"

"No. More or less, there are four of us remaining in this battle."

"More or less, four?"

"Come out from the shadows and you have my word I won't kill you until you're ready for battle. Do you require food or water or rest?"

Reggie stepped into the diffused light of the labyrinth's center. A horrific battle had ensued by the telltale blood splatter on the walls and ground. She kept her back to the wall and surveyed the center of the arena. Dog Boy looked up from a crouched position. He was wounded. He licked an injured paw. She fought the urge to run to him, to help him, to hold him. No...this wasn't the time nor place. Her feelings would betray her if she didn't bury them.

Hundi seemed unaffected by her appearance. *Sly dog. I must look frightful, covered in the black blood of a Sang, and he barely casts me a second glance.* Smart dog.

There was something more frightful than the blood-spattered walls and her own blood-soaked body. The crying. The weeping sound...it came from the Wastelander. The one who was to die last. Malik's wife by virtue of having broken her hymen.

Her head had been grafted onto the strong, broad right shoulder of her husband.

"The labyrinth has a sense of humor," the Beachling said. "We're wed in society's eyes, thereby, we fight as one in the arena."

"And how has that worked for you?"

"Did you not see the corridor leading to this place?"

"I did."

"My hands. Her teeth. She is mad. She has no sense of self. She hungers for death, but clings to life. When the mist came upon us, and we were merged, her mind could not embrace the change." The Beachling paused. "You fought a Sang, did you not? I see the tar-black blood and I smell his death upon you."

"I cut his throat with my belt buckle and pulled his head from his shoulders," Reggie admitted. Her belly churned. *I wanted to help him.*

"I salute your strength and ingenuity. Ours will be a glorious battle. I shall enjoy capturing your final breath before I rip out your eyes and skull-fuck you."

Reggie moved closer to Hundi, her gaze still fixed on the bizarre Beachling with his misshapen wife's head attached to his shoulders. "I assume you aren't prepared to live the remainder of your life with the twisted bust of a Wastelander growing from your clavicle."

"I shall have the head surgically removed." He hissed. "When I'm victorious, I'll be refused nothing."

"How much of your body and hers have connected? Do you share one heart? Do you have independent brains? I wonder...can you fuck yourself?"

The Wastelander bride snarled and drooled. Her eyes expressed more than words ever could. Eyes that begged to be dispatched.

Malik ran the tip of his blade against the ground. Little sparks appeared where the blade kissed marble. "I have the strength of two, Zoner. I respect you. Thereby, when I kill you, I hope you die well."

Reggie called upon her sight to show her a path to victory. She saw a gazelle leap and a bird's beak strike. Then the road lay clear ahead of her. For a moment, grief dealt her a heavy blow, for Hundi hadn't been included in the vision. No matter. A split second passed. Malik continued to posture, but not attack. *Is he waiting for me to move? So be it!*

She lunged at the Beachling, easily deflecting his first blow while putting her full force into a body slam. He didn't fall. She hadn't expected him to. Reggie shimmied up his torso and swung her weight around his broad shoulders as he frantically flailed about. She wrapped her strong right arm around his throat and held it in place with her left hand. And squeezed.

The stench of the Wastelander's saliva-drenched face sickened her. The pitiable lost-cow maw emanating from the woman's throat cast a frightening sound. Malik's rough, strong hands pulled at her arm. She gripped her own left forearm with her right hand and called upon a strength so deep it could have sprang from the bottom of a well. And held on. A classic wrestling move. The "sleeper hold." Always effective. Even beasts like Malik had to breathe.

Malik's already bluish face grew violet as he gasped for air.

He struck at Reggie with his blade.

She wasn't about to examine the injury. The sharp sword made a clean slice. It was barely felt. Until the warm blood seeped from her thigh where steel had kissed it. It rolled down her leg and off her foot. She envisioned a slow trickle pooling on the floor, mixing with the remains of the eleven dead combatants.

Malik took her injured leg in his free hand. He found the wound and pressed hard against it. Reggie screamed and lost concentration. He maneuvered himself from her hold, and in one solid toss, sent her flying across the vestibule.

She hit the wall shoulder first and landed in a heap. She tried to focus on Malik and nothing else. Not the pain. Not the gore and body parts surrounding her. Not Hundi.

The Beachling fought for air. Huge, full gulps. His barrel chest expanded with life-giving oxygen. His bride cackled maniacally above his rising chest.

Reggie hadn't moved. *Does he think me dead? Or at least unconscious? Can I use this to my advantage?*

She dared not feel for her knife. She wished she had her staff. *This is a bare-knuckle death match. And I must take him down.*

The songs of a hero hummed as she caught her breath and planned her next move. *What use is a sword against stone? What use is a sword against fire? Crush the stone. Smother the fire. Strike a blow to the bellows and see the hearth in the mountain fail as the mountain, itself, crumbles.*

Malik laughed. "The dead don't sweat, Zoner. Are you hot for me or for the dog I've hobbled? Shall I open you up like a spring blossom as I cut your throat? Your blood smells so sweet."

"Leave her be," Hundi said.

"The pup speaks?" Malik turned his attention to the injured Hundi. "Do you wish to see more of your body split open? Perhaps I shall pull your lungs out through your ribcage."

The bride laughed.

"Ah, she agrees. It's a good plan. First, I'll finish you and then I shall split the Zoner in half with my cock and bleed her like a pig."

"Leave…" Hundi began. He pulled himself up. "Her alone." He stood, balanced on his one good leg. He'd shifted to full human form.

"No, Hundi. Change back. You can't defeat him as a man," Reggie called.

Hundi smiled. "We shall see."

Malik turned to fully face Hundi. "I tire of this! Come at me now, dog. Or send the Zoner back into the brawl, for I need to take a piss, and the stench of this place overwhelms me."

His back was to her.

An advantage, at last. A single advantage with which to get the upper hand. She looked at her right hand. Empty. Weaponless. Small enough to be swallowed whole by the gargantuan Malik. *Swallowed whole. I do have a weapon. The one thing I've always believed in and been able to count upon. My right fist.*

"Malik!" She forced herself to her feet.

He didn't bother turning. "What do you want, girl?"

"The dog is my lover."

Hundi shook his head. "No, Reggie…"

"I don't care if it's true or false. If it's the truth she speaks, then you can enter the afterlife together," Malik replied.

Reggie took a defensive stance. "I insist that you observe your own customs before you attack. It's only fitting that before you strike my lover and send him to the afterlife that you perform the death call of the Beachlings. It ensures him better odds at being reborn into a higher caste. Surely your gods will open the gates at the sound of your cry."

"He doesn't deserve the courtesy." Malik still hadn't turned.

The heroes of her flesh prickled. *I've got this under control. Stop pushing me.* Reggie rubbed her arms to rid herself of the goose bumps. "It's my final request before conceding."

The bride gasped and twittered.

Malik turned. "You'll concede victory to me?"

Reggie nodded. Her eyes flashed at Hundi. *Please let him see I have a plan…*

"You shall die as warriors."

"Make the cry, Malik. Send us to our next lifetimes with the promise that we shall fight again," she pleaded.

Malik laughed. "Dog, stand by your woman."

Hundi circled Malik, snarling. He took a position close to Reggie. She shook off his touch.

"You won't embrace me before we meet death?" Hundi asked.

Reggie didn't take her gaze off Malik. "I wouldn't be fettered as I cross the mountains of death."

Malik laughed. "She refuses you, dog! She looks like a fighter, but she's just another woman with a woman's changeable mind. She takes you to her bed, but won't cross into death with you at her side. I love it!"

Keep laughing...keep laughing, you blue idiot. Reggie slowly closed her right hand into a fist as tightly as she could. Blood loss had taken a toll. Her hand was numb. Her vision dimmed and the room seemed askew. Malik's large head and wide-open maw were in her sights. She saw only him. His gob. His wide-open mouth.

Ignoring the numbness and fatigue, she sprang forward. She envisioned the juggernaut force of the Fire Zoner who had attacked her. A maelstrom of fury.

Malik laughed at her attack. A bold belly laugh. Head back, mouth open.

Perfect.

Hundi reached out for her but missed. She felt his warm hand against her back as she moved away.

Reggie landed a solid blow to the Beachling's face and rammed her fist into his mouth. She clung to him like a burr and forced it and then her forearm down his throat. His sharpened teeth tore her flesh. Tears welled in her eyes as the pain moved deeper and deeper into her epidermis. Newly healed flesh. Now scarred and torn.

"Hundi...the bride!" she cried, her gaze fixed on the eyes of the Wastelander.

"Aye, beloved!"

In one fluid movement, he shifted from man to wolf-dog and leaped into action, his sharp teeth snapping shut on the bride's throat. She and Reggie had fixed gazes as Hundi's jaws took her life and Malik succumbed to lack of oxygen. She held the bride's gaze and watched as the spirit of the woman took flight. A brilliant yellow flash popped at the moment of her death. It rose and cascaded down just as quickly, her suffering fading away like fireflies at dawn.

Buried up to her elbow, Reggie fell upon Malik as he collapsed. A moment later, he was dead.

Hundi rallied to her side.

A low hum of applause and victory cries wafted, welled up from the marble floors, pools of blood and broken bodies.

Hundi shifted, and carefully, gingerly, helped Reggie extract her arm from Malik's split mouth. She'd broken his jaw. Suffocated him. The smell of his demise nearly overpowered her. His stink far outweighed the already pervasive air of the chamber.

She winced as the last of her hand came free. "It looks like a freshly plowed field. The furrows made by teeth into flesh. My soil bleeds red." The cold chill of shock enveloped her.

"Please, let me bind your wounds. Otherwise you'll bleed out." He examined her leg wound. "Oh, steam…this is deep." He reached out and ripped off a portion of clothing from a dead fighter and then wrapped her leg and forearm. "You won't lose any fingers. Truthfully, it's only your arm that's injured. Good call, Reggie. Getting him to open his mouth…brilliant."

With an impulsive move, Reggie pulled Hundi's mouth to hers. "Thank you. Are you all right?"

Hundi nodded. "I'll lose part of a foot, but I'm otherwise intact."

"What do we do with them? Leave them for the caretakers to find?"

Hundi pulled Reggie to her feet. "This isn't the time for remorse or rituals. They're fighters who died in combat. There are no words that can even come close to the glory of their deaths." He paused. "Can you walk?"

She took a few steps. "I can ignore pain. I can shake off shock and banish hunger and thirst. I'm ready to make tracks away from this bright center of the universe."

"There is something else we could do first. Before moving on. Before the caretakers arrive." He patted the altar stone. "I would take you here. Now."

"No, Hundi…it's I who shall take you. I promised you this." Reggie placed her palms against the marble block and pulled her weight up.

Hundi moved between her legs. "I give myself to you."

"Hundi, I ran into a Sang after falling into the vortex. Although I defeated him in the end, he had his way with me while I was unconscious. He wanted me to stay and produce labyrinth-born children. A mother to the lost souls who feed this place in between battles."

"If you hadn't killed him, it would become my life's mission to see him laid to waste."

"He bit me. On my thigh. If I'm infected by the spit and seed of a Sang…"

"My seed is stronger than that of any vampire. Let me fill you and give you such pleasure that the pain he caused shall become null and void in your heart and mind. Should a child grow inside you, rest assured, it'll be mine — not his."

Reggie could not express her agreement deeply

enough. "Yes. Yes. I want you to burn the scum of that Sang bastard from me, and when I look back on this day, remember only your touch. I shall never think of him again. I shall never speak his name. His violent acts end here."

Hundi pulled off her breeches and then opened his. "The bite marks are fresh, but not deep. I don't see how he could have infected you with such a shallow taste."

Reggie reclined, allowing Hundi to pull her forward. "I offered to be his first meal. His turning point. He was too eager. Alone for too long."

She winced as Hundi positioned his thick cock to take her. The Sang had bruised her. Hundi would heal her.

She stretched her arms out above her head to grip the edge of the altar. He leaned forward and thrust with all his might. Her clitoris twitched at the aggressive sex.

Reggie arched her back and moaned. She wrapped her legs around Hundi's torso. "Harder! More!" she cried. "Destroy any part of me that is rat-bastard semi-Sang. I don't want his scent or his seed on me any longer."

Hundi climaxed, his back arched and his head thrown back. He spilled, then pulled away and howled. Though wearing his manskin, his wolf's cry echoed in the vestibule of the labyrinth and coursed out into the labyrs and lunations.

Reggie sobbed as the throes of their passion subsided.

Hundi stroked Reggie's matted hair. "A fighter doesn't cry at times such as these, my love. This is a time to rejoice. A time to reflect on the events that left you alive and led you to this place."

"We make love in carnage. I killed a Sang I wanted only to help. I feel regret."

Hundi lifted Reggie off the altar stone. "We stand at the center of the great labyrinth of Ironhedge-Ghillie. The center of a labyrinth, in a classical sense, stands for beauty, love, formation, and transformation. We're a part of these things, Reggie. You're so beautiful to me. A child may have been sired by the Sang within you, but now my potency shall transform any spark of life from a child of darkness to a child of light. And, Reggie, I love you. I've loved you since you bested me over the fire pit at the Clockworx."

"I love you, too. But Hundi, you're forgetting that we must battle. You and I. Only one of us can leave this place."

"I challenge their rules."

Reggie touched his face thoughtfully. "As do I. I have grown quite fond of you, my friend. I feel inklings of what can only be love, in fact. I would explore a deeper relationship with you once we are free of this place. Tell me, Hundi, what is your wish? If you're victorious, what dream would you see come true?"

"Name your desire first."

"I would see my brother released from the Sang brothel where he's indentured for gambling debts."

"A noble wish."

"What's yours?" she asked again.

"I would see your brother released from the brothel."

Reggie covered her face with her hands and wept.

CHAPTER FOURTEEN

"**I** don't deserve your love, Hundi." She wiped her face with the back of her hand.

"You earned my love. You have my heart and respect. And if you scratch behind my ears now and then, you'll earn—"

"I get the picture." She affectionately patted his arm. "I'm not a nice person. I'm sarcastic, I generally leave a trail of destruction in my wake, and I'm so without compassion for the lives of others I can have sex surrounded by the stinking dead. I paid the elevator attendant for a bit of oral, for steam's sake."

Hundi smiled slyly. "So did I."

Reggie burst into laughter mid-swallow and choked. "You didn't."

Hundi nodded. "I did."

"And more, my friend, I think I'm unwell. The bite of the Sang has, indeed, affected me. I feel odd," Reggie continued.

"Hunger. Thirst. These things we can fight," Hundi replied. "Even a fighter such as yourself must rest and eat and drink. That's all you need."

I'm thirsty, but I dare not say aloud that which I crave. "Yes. Perhaps." She took a deep breath, relishing the pungent, acrid odor of spilled blood. *Graham got me. Not only do I fear pregnancy by that rot bastard, I can tell his spittle has infected me. I'm changing. Damn it.*

The sound of iron to stone drew their attention. The pitch was hollow and shrill, and sent a cold shiver over Reggie's spine. "The caretakers."

"Or worse." Hundi palmed his short blade.

The gooseflesh on Reggie's arms tingled and danced.

The message of the heroes was clear. *Fighters, flee from this decay and live to fight another day.*

Hundi touched her left arm. "I heard that."

"Apparently what comes next frightens even the heroes. And they're dead. We're urged to flee." Reggie backed around to the far side of the altar stone.

Hundi took a defense stance. "It grows hot and the stench of the fallen unbearable."

Reggie laughed. A hard laugh. Out of place. Nervous. *I like the smell of the decay permeating this place. I'm turning. I feel the surge of the Sang in my gut.* "Whatever approaches, whatever fate awaits us as we make our way out, we mustn't back down. I choose to stay to see what beast drags its sword our way." *Am I so ready to die? If I'm to be Sang, then I'm already living a half-life. My head lopped off my shoulders might be my saving grace.*

Oppressive, thick, uncomfortable steam

cascaded into the center. The clang continued. The steam moved with the sound.

"I don't know what that is," Reggie whispered. "It's steam, yes…but it's more than that."

"It's powerful. I feel its heat and strength of purpose in my bones. It frightens me, Reggie. I know what it is…" Hundi paused. "It's God."

"God?" Reggie asked. "Which god? Steam?"

"Yes. Steam. We stand in the presence of Steam. With a capital S. The life-giving vapors that run the IG and helped our world rise from the ashes." Hundi covered his eyes.

"There is no divinity in steam." She pulled Hundi's hand away from his face. "Be strong, fighter." She paused, regretfully realizing what power might approach. "This is our final battle. No doubt the rage-ravenous spirit of this place needs to participate somehow to become fully sated. Besides that, I think she's here for me. I offended her when I killed the Sang. He called her the Mother. I guess I broke Mama's toy."

"You defended yourself. There is no shame in that. My love…I shall stand beside you in battle."

"I'm not sure how to fight something that feeds on torment and the suffering and deaths of others. Will it grow more powerful if we raise arms against it? Will we be mowed down if we turn our backs?"

Hundi braced himself on his one good foot and put his long blade at the ready. "Time to dance, beloved. She has arrived."

CHAPTER FIFTEEN

Reggie gagged as the unlikely all-powerful spirit of the arena wafted into the center of the labyrinth. Hundi turned to vomit. The odor permeating the spirit of the arena came from beyond the grave. Beyond blood. Beyond the sweat of battle.

The spirit of the labyrinth wore Graham's head on a chain, which trailed out behind her like a bride's veil in a macabre weave of severed body parts. Old, desiccated. Skeletal. And like Graham's, some fresh. She stood tall and opaque—in most places. A tattered white dress reminiscent of a prewar bridal gown hung on her frame like a woman who'd lost too much weight too quickly.

The stand-off fed the already thick anxiety in the air.

Thicker was the powerful surge of half-life, of Sang, of wanton blood fever. It shook Reggie's core. It made her want to fight. Fight a god. If the essence of Sang enhanced one's most base qualities—then truly, her prowess in battle had increased tenfold.

"You don't look all that omnipotent. What's with the jewelry of the damned?" she asked.

Hundi struck her arm softly. "Don't, Reggie."

"I'm not afraid of her. So far, the worst I've seen her do is humiliate the queen by making him wear a penis gourd. *Ooooo…wicked.*"

The husky, dull-faced, steely-eyed woman blocking the entrance said nothing. Broad shoulders draped with dusty lace squared and her posture grew rigid, but she didn't attack.

She doesn't have to speak. Reggie picked up the sword of one of the fallen. "I know why you're here. And you know what? I'd do it again," she boasted. "Rip off the head of an enemy? Break your toy? In a heartbeat. Even a pitiable one like that Sang. I'll kill any man who believes he has the right to take liberties with my body. I'm not afraid to kill or die."

The gruesomely decorated woman made no response. Not even a blink or smirk.

"Make your move, you soggy demi-goddess," Reggie said. She cursed under her breath. "I hate steam. Give me the desert any day."

The spirituous being raised a single finger toward them. A single finger. "You don't understand why I'm here, or why I've been here or why I must continue *here*. However, no deed can go unrewarded or punished. This is for killing my companion," she said.

Her voice came at them like a winter gale. A blast so violent in force it nearly toppled them.

Daggers of air stabbed and ripped at their already injured flesh. Reggie screeched as a shard of sharp air lodged in her left eye.

She let forth with a stream of curse words that could make the most debased pack of dog boys blush. Blood poured into her eye. Blinded, she let it flow. She took a moment, only a moment, to fight back the pain and bury the shock. She pulled herself erect, refusing to allow pain to conquer her. She hadn't released the short sword taken from the corpse of a fallen comrade. She postured aggressively and licked her blood from her lips.

"Tastes like victory. The wine of triumph."

She shuddered. *Wine, indeed. Intoxicating, sweet wine.* Her mouth watered for another taste, but not her own. The carnage around her, on the floor and walls and bodies of the fallen, made her thirst. The bite marks on her inner thigh throbbed. Her heart beat fast—and then a great calm fell over her. *I'm Sang. I must feed.*

Hundi rose and moved in close beside Reggie. "My love…are you able to continue?"

Reggie nodded, the gaze of her single eye fixed. "More ready than ever before."

Hundi took a step forward, partially shielding Reggie. "She has grown more…substantial."

Reggie agreed. "She gains strength as we bleed out."

The entity spoke. "Return the songs of the heroes that you've stolen from me and I'll forgive you for beheading my pet. You'll get to keep your other eye."

"I've stolen nothing." Reggie paused and exhaled. She wiped the blood from her blinded eye.

The shard remained. So did her temper. The pain just made her angry. "What kind of spirit are you to feed on the suffering of others? You mock the queen and tormented the Sang into lunacy. You demand fealty of blood, and must be pacified less you engage the whole of the world in your hunger pangs. You've made it so a woman can't haggle over the price of a chicken in the market. You're ridiculous."

"You have no idea how much worse things would be without me and my hunger for the lesser selves of humanity. Without me chaos would reign. I'm the tarnished side of the coin, the cloud covering the sun. I'm needed, and have been put asunder for too long. It wasn't I who muzzled buyers in the market, Zoner—that was Viktor. He's a liar. He binds me to this place and shackles me with laws and restrictive rules of etiquette. Now, his chains are like spider's silk. Easily broken. He says I torment him? He does those things to himself. He starves me. I hunger for the bickering of lovers, the sham of the seller and curses of a buyer."

The spirit paused, exhaling a soft puff of steam that formed a decorative pattern in the air. "If you want to see a real monster, look to your queen. He has done more harm than good. I need battle and blood. Despair and hopelessness are so sweet against my lips the moment before the sword strikes. I love war. I love strife. What doesn't kill you makes me stronger. Makes humanity and hybrid kinds stronger, but Viktor, the queen, wishes nothing but utter control over your lives. Ultimate control. Over your words, thoughts and deeds. Over your body. Over your orgasms. Freedom has no meaning in his world. He has made me a god in the eyes of the people when I'm much more than a simple deity. I'm the embodiment of the most fundamental elements on the planet. Steam isn't divine. It's pure energy. If I were free, and Viktor ruled no longer, rest assured balance would return to the world. You'd certainly have the privilege of haggling over chicken should my shackles be removed. And there would be justice again. Justice for all—even those like your brother, who is forced to pay his debt in blood. Yes…he would go free. All those tormented souls living outside the rules of society would be freed from tyranny. I tell you, Zoner…in every man there is a fighter, and in every fighter there is a hero. In every hero there is a song. This is why I can't allow you to pass imbued with their songs. Their voices would be lost on one person when they belong here. Their song fortifies the labyrinth. Viktor would silence them. He keeps the people blind and deaf to the glories of free thought, debate and personal victory. Did you know it's he who authorized blood debt? He doesn't care about the people so long as no one raises a voice above a whisper."

Reggie's flesh prickled. A hero chimed out. *Sense she makes. Lives at stake.* She shook off the vibration of the songs of her flesh and called upon her inner sight. She saw her own shadow cast against the bloody marble of the arena.

"I was taken by force in a foul and vile manner by your insane plaything and you stand here now attempting to make me feel sorry for you? Your

Sang wished me to be the mother of labyrinth-born children. What mother would suffer a child to be born into this hellish place? And why?" Reggie exhaled and caught Hundi's arm for support. "Let us pass."

"I can't," the spirit said. "I need the songs of your flesh returned. And Graham curried favor in many ways. He was always unstable, but he provided me with companionship, and he will be missed."

Hundi spat. "Missed so dearly you wear his severed head?"

"Viktor controls the burdens I bear. Now, Zoner…I need the heroes' voices returned. It's important."

"And I need my humanity restored! The Sang bit me." Reggie paused. "Move aside or I swear I shall cap your vent and let your fire burn itself out. I can *see* you. I see right through you."

The spirit shook her head. "Hybrid fighter, look harder. See the truth."

"No!" a voice rang out. It echoed. It carried panic. It pulsed with fear.

Hundi whispered, "It's the queen. Viktor. He approaches."

Reggie ignored Hundi. She ignored the plaintive cry of the queen as he sashayed into the center of the arena, muscling his way past the steamy spirit.

Viktor wore cotton-duct pants and a high-collar silk shirt. Vintage articles. Not unflattering. "Fighter…um…Rachel…"

"It's Reggie."

"Yes. Reggie. And Houndi."

"Hundi."

Viktor waved off the correction. "Reggie. Hundi. Don't believe a word this antediluvian ghost says. She's the great trickster. I've come to rescue you from her evil clutches."

Reggie laughed. "Where were you when my arm was up to elbow in the Beachling's gob? Or when the steam-bitch here blinded me? Or when I was raped by a Sang?"

Viktor tried to touch Reggie. She shook him off. "Reggie…you didn't need assistance at those times. I'm here to escort you out as winner. We shall retrieve your brother and give you a fine parade."

"Why do you think I need assistance now?"

"You're being deceived. You're a very special young woman, and I can't allow you to be further abused."

Hundi squeezed Reggie's upper arm. "I don't believe him," he whispered.

"I'm one who fought, nothing more. Why am I special to you now, Viktor?" Reggie asked.

"You've been anointed with the essence of all those who came before you. The knowledge carried in your veins is…unprecedented. I would see the institution of a new seat on the council. The heroes of your flesh—their songs can only enhance the laws of the land. This has been a most startling battle. I can restore your eyesight, you know. If that's your wish, my champion. All you need do is come with me. Now. She can't harm you in my presence."

"I don't need you to restore my eyesight," Reggie replied. *My hybrid sight combined with the sleek vision of my new Sang abilities…it's all good. I can see things quite plainly. My path is clear. I'm shadow.*

I'm Sang. And that's how I shall win.

The heroes of her flesh rallied in support. *Life through unlife to end the strife.*

Through the throbbing in her forehead, Reggie heard the songs of the heroes. *They are telling me how to win.* She relaxed her stance. "I tire of this."

Hundi went agape. "What? What?"

Reggie held a finger aloft to silence Hundi. "We concede. We aren't going to engage in any activity that will please either of you."

The spirit's face grew pinched and sour. "Return the heroes to me."

Reggie laughed. "I won't."

"Pledge allegiance to me and I shall lead you safely from this place," Viktor commanded.

Reggie shook her head. "No." She turned to Hundi. "Do you trust me, my love?"

"Implicitly," he replied.

She struck before Hundi had a chance to lift his blade.

Her sword slashed his throat, and he fell, a look of utter surprise on his face.

He reached out for her. His voice gone. He gurgled his last words. Air bubbles welled up from the wound and his blood flowed, thick and hot. It perfumed the air.

Reggie dropped to her knees and pressed her lips to Hundi's throat. Her tongue darted out to taste the nectar. Delicious. Nourishing. *I'm Sang.*

She drank deeply. Beneath her, Hundi died.

Reggie stood as the last pulse of life fled Hundi's still-warm corpse. She wiped her mouth with the back of her hand. "I'm the last fighter standing. I'm victorious."

The spirit of the arena grew dim. "You don't understand, fighter…"

"I will have my reward now," Reggie said sharply to Viktor, who'd taken on the stance of a small child in need of a restroom.

Viktor nodded. "That's your right. What, may I ask, do you wish? As I said, I'll kill myself, here and now, if that's your pleasure. I can't go back on my word. Especially not here. In this place."

Reggie laughed. "It'd please me greatly to see you walk head-on into the carnivorous garden I passed on my way here, but that isn't the reward I crave."

Viktor took a deep breath. An obvious sigh of relief. "Name it."

Reggie took a moment and wrapped her right hand with a piece of cloth torn from the tunic of a fallen combatant. She pulled the shard from her left eye and cast it aside. She didn't flinch.

"Firstly, I'd see the spirit of this place released from her bonds."

The spirit gasped.

Viktor slammed his right fist against the blood-spattered wall. "No!"

"You can deny me nothing as victor. I further request that the heroes be returned to the walls of this place, for it's they who are the true spirits of the labyrinth. They belong here. Not with me."

Viktor replied, his voice hoarse. "It isn't so easily done."

Reggie rushed Viktor and cornered him. "It had better be."

HUNDI STIRRED. HE slowly opened his eyes. He heard Reggie's demands. Through death's fog he watched. A flicker of warmth coursed through his body. Her voice echoed as his final thoughts surfaced. "Do you trust me?"

Implicitly.

Viktor clapped his hands. A seemingly innocuous motion followed by a startling event.

His head in a fog, his heart racing, he witnessed the heroes rise from Reggie's flesh as if she were a caterpillar and they butterflies, emerging from silken chrysalis.

Cirrus of smoke wafted into the walls. A choir of voices joined together and then dissipated into the marble walls and floor of the center of the great labyrinth.

Viktor broke down and wept.

Reggie scoffed at the display of weakness.

The spirit shimmered and laughed. Her shackles fell away.

Viktor screeched as the spirit swept over him.

Together, they vanished.

* * * *

Viktor stomped his foot. "I won't be a part of this!"

The more corporeal entity smiled softly. "You are queen."

"I resign."

"You have no female heir. Perhaps it's time you took a wife."

"I don't want a wife!" Viktor hit the wall again. "My perfect society…all gone."

"Perfection breeds imperfection, Viktor. Let

nature take its course. You must learn the compassion of a mother to her children. You can't control. You must embrace." The spirit of the arena kneeled and took Viktor into her arms.

The queen sobbed. "There will be war. You'll grow too strong. Civility will perish. Steam will be replaced and engines of destruction will rule."

"You know that isn't so, Viktor. I made it possible for compassion and love to house the more aggressive tendencies of the people. In your fear, and I'm sorry…your delusions…you usurped the grand plan of Steam and Mother. I'm the darkness before dawn's rise, the winter before spring. The world can heal now, my son. You must grow up and be the queen I know you can be."

The queen sighed. "No more penis gourds and fish hooks?"

The spirit shook her head. "No. It's time for crown and scepter."

Viktor stood. "I'm sorry, Mother. I've behaved quite badly."

* * * *

Hundi sat upright as a potent surge of life force rejuvenated him. "Reggie," he whispered. "Do we live?"

She went to his side and kissed him. "No, beloved. Not exactly."

"I taste blood upon your lips," Hundi said. "It is the blood of our shared enemy?"

"It's yours."

"I see. The bite of the Sang was deeper than we

thought. You *turned* and then you *made* me."

"We're Sang. It was the only way."

Hundi nodded. "I understand. If I am to live a great long life because of my new heritage, at least I shall spend it with you."

Reggie helped him to his feet. "I love you, Hundi."

He straightened his clothing. "And I you. Everything is going to change now, I think."

"I know it is." Reggie held his hand and led him toward the long path to the exit. "Let's get out of here. I feel hard-pressed to haggle over the price of a chicken."

EPILOGUE

Three full moons had passed.

Reggie darted outside.

She barely noticed the golden sunrise as she vomited into the waste bin at the rear exit of her dwelling. As she heaved, she tried not to knock over the morning delivery of the good stuff. The red stuff. Two loaves of piping hot bread had been delivered too. Nothing like chewy peasant bread to dip into one's morning beverage.

These were good times in the Zone. Barely three months had passed since her victory in the labyrinth, and the ripple effect of the new regime had proved beneficial. She glanced at her brother's window. A gentle light flickered. *He's awake.*

She still didn't pray, but if ever there was something to be thankful about, it was him. Her twin brother. Alive, well and not Sang.

"Are you unwell, beloved?" Hundi asked as Reggie wandered back inside.

She pulled up a chair and sat by their bed. "My ulcer," Reggie replied.

"Shall I retrieve that white elixir that calms your stomach?"

She shook her head. "No, thank you."

Hundi patted the bed, inviting her to return. "You sang in your sleep again. It reminds me of when we were in the arena and the songs of your flesh entertained me while you were unconscious."

"You're the only thing that makes my flesh sing, Hundi." Reggie thought of crawling back into bed and using Hundi roughly, but turned aside to become ill once again. Dry heaves.

"Please let me take you to the village physician," Hundi said.

"No doctors." Reggie crawled back into bed. "No doctors, ever. I don't trust them."

Hundi reached out to massage her aching belly. Reggie played with his thick blond hair.

In the calm stillness of the morning, a melody rose. "Hundi, you make me miss the heroes with your humming."

"It isn't I who hums. I thought it was you."

Reggie jumped to her feet, her hand over her belly. She closed her right eye, for she wore an eye patch over her left, and called upon her sight. The path revealed to her brought tears to her eye. What she saw exposed was her greatest adventure yet to come.

The songs of the flesh continue…inside me. I am with child. "Oh, Hundi…"

"If it isn't I, nor is it you — and we both know your brother can't carry a tune — who sings?" Hundi asked.

"Our baby sings," Reggie replied. "The songs of the flesh are now…*hers*…"

ABOUT THE AUTHOR

Darragha Foster enjoys the twisted and unusual. She finds inspiration all around her. Even in the cold case at the grocer…where she is no longer welcome. But that's another story…

Links to find Darragha Foster:

Website: http://www.darragha.com/

Author Facebook:
https://www.facebook.com/DarraghaFoster/

Darragha also write urban fantasy under the name JJ Andrews